# Stalked

*A Sweet Stalker Collection*

Hope Ford

# Stalking Her

Hope Ford

# Chapter 1

## *Brooke*

I have a stalker.

I should be scared. I should probably tell someone. But I'm not going to. It would be different if I thought he wanted to hurt me. But I'm pretty sure he doesn't. As a matter of fact, I think he wants me.

I'm trying not to be obvious, but it's impossible. I'm searching for him and won't be satisfied until I get to see him. It's like I feel agitated and on edge and I don't know why. He's a stranger. Well, mostly. This is the third Saturday in a row that I've come to Blaze. It's a night club, and night clubs are not my thing.

I'm an attorney; actually, I just recently graduated law school and have just started at Simon, Schwartz, and Teller. I have my first big case coming up in a few months, and I should be home preparing, but instead I'm here with two women from the office. They are attorneys but have more experience than me. The first time they asked me to come with them, I agreed because I knew I needed to play nice with my coworkers. But now, I'm coming for a completely different reason.

Lane Davis. He's a bouncer. Head security for Blaze. I noticed him the first time I came here, and he watched me every second. Every move I made, his eyes were on me.

"That one's cute," Brenda says, interrupting my thoughts when she points at a man standing a few feet away. "And there's three of them," she says happily.

I barely resist rolling my eyes. Brenda and Cassie are both tall and thin. If they ever decide to quit their day job, they could quite literally make a living as models. And then there's me. I'm short and curvy and their exact opposite. She always finds three guys for us to dance with, and I hate seeing the disappointed look on the third one's face when he discovers that he didn't get Brenda or Cassie. No, he got me. The short, frumpy one.

"Yeah, cute," I remark, just so they don't notice that I could care less about the three clean-cut guys they're looking at. I'm in search of my tall, dark, tattooed stalker.

Lane's never said a word to me. He still hasn't. But he's so far under my skin it doesn't even matter. After the first time I saw him, the next day I noticed him at the grocery store. Since then, I've seen him outside my office, my apartment building, and the gym. He never says a word. Just watches me.

I freaked out a little bit at first and can admit I was scared. I know he could have been a psycho or something, but my gut was telling me different. I called Blaze, and with the description I gave them, they were able to give me his name. He's head of security, and I have no doubt it would get back to him that I was asking about him, but I didn't care. I had to know.

Next, I called my sister-in-law. She's a police officer, and I knew she would help me. I didn't tell her why but asked her to look into him. She asked me what all I needed to know, and I told her anything she could find. Well, she didn't disappoint. She came back to me in less than an hour. Lane Davis, thirty-two years old, no criminal record. He received a parking ticket three years ago but looks like it was paid the same day it was issued. He's divorced. Finalized two years ago. Records indicate infidelity.

I texted her back, holding my breath. "He cheated?"

And her response was immediate. "No. She cheated."

From that moment on, I decided to go with my gut. Lane is nothing like the men I've dated in the past. He's not clean-cut. He's not goofy or vain or way too into himself. No, it seems he's way into me. And that's why I'm here at Blaze again. I'm going to get him to talk to me one way or another.

I look at the door that leads to the back, and suddenly he appears. He doesn't look around like he usually does; his gaze goes straight to me, and I melt in my seat. I swear when he looks at me it's like he's burning a hole in me. Instead of blushing and looking away like I normally do, I look at him as if I'm challenging him. How can I convey in a look that I want him to talk to me? Heck, I will take anything with him.

He crosses his arms over his chest and stares right back.

I feel a nudge in my side and a whispered yell in my ear. "They're coming over."

Reluctantly, I drag my gaze from Lane and look at the three preppy guys in the button-down shirts as they walk toward the table.

All three of them are looking between Brenda and Cassie, which is fine because I want to look at Lane. I'm about to excuse myself and walk over when Lane touches his ear, like he's listening to something from the earpiece, and turns quickly on his feet. He walks three feet in the opposite direction before turning to look at me. Even from across the room with a fleeting look, he commands all my attention. I know that look. It's almost like I can feel him saying it in my ear. *Don't move.*

Too bad I'm not a girl that listens because it hits me then... I know how I'm going to get him to talk to me. Every time someone has asked me to dance, I've said no. Well, not today. No, today I'm going to the dance floor. If he doesn't like it, he'll have to come and get me. And damn do I want him to come and get me.

"All right – so who wants to dance?" I ask.

Brenda and Cassie are immediately out of their seats and grabbing on to the guys that are closest to them. The man in the middle at least has the decency to hide his disappointment as he waits for me to come around the table.

He puts his hand at the small of my back, and I pick up speed. Maybe this wasn't such a good idea after all. Him dancing with me is one thing. Him touching me is another.

The music is loud and bumping, and I can't keep from moving if I try. I look over my dance partner's shoulder and all around for a glance of Lane. Then I look up on the balcony, but he's nowhere to be seen. Determined and knowing he can be looking at me from anywhere in the club, watching me right now, I dance. I dip my hips, shake my butt, and let the music move me. I'm all but lost in the song when I feel hands on my hips. My whole body freezes. My dance partner has moved up on me and is grinding against me. I pull away, and knowing he can't hear me, I shake my head side to side, letting him know that I don't want him to touch me.

I continue to dance, but with less butt shaking. When the man reaches for me again, this time I stop and make sure he can hear me. "I'm not interested."

I look at Brenda and Cassie, and they're dancing with their partners, so I walk off. I'm going to go to the ladies' room and then to get another drink. I'm almost to the bathroom when I'm pulled in the opposite direction and backed into a wall.

It takes me a second to catch my breath, but when I do, I'm pushing against the asshole's chest. "I told you I'm not interested."

But he's not letting me loose. He uses his body to hold me against the wall, and I can feel his hard manhood pressed into my belly. I feel sick and try to push him off me. People are walking by, but to them it probably looks like we're making out. He's so much bigger than me, I can't do anything but relax my body and give him the idea that I'm into it. Only then does he loosen his hold enough to lean back so he can look into my face. As soon as he lets his guard down, I give him a shove and then punch him in the face.

I try to keep wailing on him, but he catches my arms. He smiles a lethal smile that tells me he's getting off on the fact that I'm fighting back. He brings his hand back, and it's then I know he's going to hit me. I clench my eyes shut as I try to wrestle away from him.

# Chapter 2

## *Lane*

My girl didn't listen. And even though I've never talked to her or even touched her, she's my girl.

There was an incident at the door, and one of the guards needed back-up. I left my spot of watching Brooke after giving her the look, telling her not to move. But she didn't listen. She and her friends are gone from they had been sitting. I look over the balcony and spot her friends, but Brooke is nowhere to be seen.

I walk through the club searching for her. I talk into the mic. "Any eyes on Angel?" That's right. They all know Brooke is mine. They've all helped me keep an eye on her just because there've been times I couldn't leave and needed to make sure she made it home safe. So everyone knows Angel, and they know she's mine.

"Fuck, Lane. I saw her go toward the bathroom, but I just got called to the bar for a skipped tab so I had to leave her." Mike's voice is on edge and it's no doubt because he knows how hung up on Angel I am.

"I got her," I grunt into the mic.

I push people in the crowd to make my way to the hallway that leads to the bathrooms. There's a lot of people, but just like any other time, I find her easily. She's struggling in the arms of a man, and I run full speed to them. "What the fuck?" I say, just as I put my hand out to stop the man from swinging and hitting her.

I recognize him as one of the yuppie assholes that was watching her earlier, and I start to pummel him without any thought to anything except making sure he's never able to touch her again.

"Lane! Stop. You're going to kill him," my Angel says as she tries to come between me and the man lying on the floor.

She puts her hand to my heaving chest. I put the mic to my mouth. "Clean up in the hallway. And make sure he learns a lesson for touching Angel."

"On it," Mike says. "She okay?"

And the fact that I can hear the concern in his voice is the only thing that's going to stop me from firing his ass. He knows how important Angel is to me, and there's supposed to be eyes on her at all times.

"Yes. She's fine. I got her."

People are all standing around, videoing and taking pictures. Brooke stands behind me. "I can't be on the news for this."

Fuck, in my endeavor to protect her, it seems I've fucked up. She's an up-and-coming attorney, and she sure as shit can't be surrounded by all of this.

"I'm leaving. Hold down the fort. I'll be back," I say into the mic as I hustle Brooke out the back door.

I stop in the alley and watch her. She's holding her hand in front of her. "You okay?"

She nods. "Yeah, I got one punch in, but obviously I'm not a fighter." She holds her hand out, and her knuckles are red and bruised.

I tense, debating on going back in there, and she must realize it because she shakes her head. "He's not worth it."

"Can I take you home?"

I wait for her to refuse. No doubt she's going to, but she surprises me when she says yes. "Let me just text Brenda and Cassie so they are on the lookout in case that guy's friends are asses too."

She takes her phone out of her back pocket and starts to text. I walk her to my truck and help her inside. She's on her phone most of the ride. "I'm sorry. They're worried about me."

"It's no problem," I tell her. Honestly, I'm glad she has friends looking out for her.

She's quiet the whole way until I'm pulling up to her apartment building.

She gets out before I can say anything, and I meet her at the front of my truck. She's still holding her hand, but she's looking at me curiously. "Are we going to talk about the fact that you know where I live?"

I debate on answering her truthfully for only a second, and then decide against it. There's nothing good that can come from the fact that I'm her stalker. But I can't lie to her. "I'd rather not."

She's watching me. She's standing so close to me her head is bent back so she can look up into my face. This is the closest we've been to each other, and I'm breathing her in, hoping to commit her vanilla sugar scent to memory.

She puts her hand on my chest. My heart is beating erratically, and I wonder if she can feel it. "Are you coming up?"

I reach up and wrap my hand around hers. It's on the tip of my tongue to tell her no when she flinches. I let her go and realize that I'd forgotten her hurt hand. "Yeah," I grunt and then clear my throat. "Yeah, I'm coming up. I'm going to take care of that hand."

She turns then, and I follow her through the door. The doorman has it open for her, and he's openly watching me in disgust. I'm sure he doesn't get a lot of men in here that are covered in tattoos. The high dollar apartment building and snooty doorman is just another sign that Brooke, my Angel, is out of my league. Regardless, I nod at him and follow Brooke into the elevator. "I'm on the fifth floor," she says, and then turns to look at me. "But you probably already know that."

I don't answer her either way. Instead I stand next to her and swear I can feel the heat coming off her body. She takes a step closer to me, and my hand that is hanging at my side brushes along her jean-clad thigh. She sucks in a breath, and I clench my eyes tightly together to refrain from taking her right now against the elevator wall.

*She's too good for you, Lane.*

The elevator dings, letting us know we have arrived just as the doors come open. I follow behind her and watch her ass swing from side to side. I've watched her walk a hundred times, and I know she's swinging her hips with more effort tonight, and I know it's just for me.

She unlocks the door and pushes it open, and I follow her in. She drops her phone and keys on the counter and looks up at me. The look on her face is so hopeful, I know I need to get out of here before I do something that I can't take back.

"May I see your hand?"

She holds it out to me instantly, and I hold it in both of mine, lifting it to the light. Luckily there is no skin broken. I push along her knuckles. "Does that hurt?"

She shakes her head. "I don't think it's broken. Just bruised."

I walk over to the freezer and peek in. After rummaging, I pull out a bag of frozen peas. "You need to put this on it so the swelling will go down."

I wrap it in a dish towel hanging from a cabinet door and gesture to the table. She sits down on the edge of her seat, and I pull a chair out and sit down next to her. She's already holding her hand out, and I gently put the frozen bag on her knuckles. "Is this okay?"

She nods, staring up at me wide-eyed.

"So I'm guessing that you know who I am," she says.

I don't want to admit I do, but yeah, I know everything about her. Her family comes from old money. Wilson, the next town over, is where she's from. Her family founded the city or some shit, and well, everyone knows who the Wilsons are. Just like anyone that knows her knows she's too good for the likes of me.

She's still looking at me. "Yeah," I mutter, "I know who you are."

She licks her lips, and I barely contain my groan. Images of her sweet, cherry lips wrapped around my cock are going through my head. My cock is lengthening in my pants, and I know I need to get out of here. I stand up, turning away from her before she sees what she's doing to me. "I need to go."

I get up quickly and start for the door when the chair screeches across the floor, and I can feel her behind me. "Wait. You don't have to go."

"I do. I should go."

"Well, let me pay you for driving me home."

That stops me, and I turn just for her to run into my chest with a loud umph. My hands go to her shoulders. "I'm not taking your money."

She blinks at my harsh tone. "I didn't... I wasn't trying to offend you."

Because I'm weak and have no control. Because she's way too good for me and all I want is one taste and I know this is my only chance, I wrap my hand around her neck and bend her head back so she's looking up at me. Her chest is heaving, and with each breath her nipples are brushing against me. "If you don't want to offend me then don't offer me money."

She bites her lip again, something I've noticed she does when she's nervous. "Fine. I just wanted to thank you."

My hand slides up her neck, and I cup her cheek. Her eyes widen, and she's staring at my lips. "You want to thank me?"

She nods slowly.

"Then let me kiss you. One kiss," I all but grunt at her.

I'm like a schoolboy, just about to blow my load in my pants, and all she's done is stare up at me. I can only imagine if I saw her without her clothes or if she touched me.

"Yes." She breathes the word heavily.

And that's all it takes. I lean down until we are only inches apart. She's staring at my lips, and I can see the hunger. She wants this. She either doesn't know or doesn't care how bad I am for her, because she wants it.

"Open your mouth," I demand.

She does what she's told. She's on her tiptoes, but I still lift her up until she's off the ground, and her legs go around my waist. Our breath is hot and mingling, but we still haven't touched. It's like a promise of exactly how good it's going to be, and fuck, I hope I'm strong enough to stop with one kiss.

"One kiss," I breathe, and as I speak, my lips peck against hers.

She moans, and it comes deep from within her chest. "Yes."

She hooks her legs tighter around me, and I pull her in closer as I touch my lips firmly to hers. I meant to take it slow, to cherish the taste of her on my lips, but instead, it's like a frenzy, and I can't get close enough. Her hands are squeezing my neck, and her breasts are smashed to my chest. She's moving in my arms, creating friction between our bodies, and still I can't stop. I take a few more seconds of the sweetest pleasure I've ever known before pulling my mouth from hers. With a sharp groan, I release her and set her back on the floor. My body has reacted like I knew it would. I'm hard, harder than I've ever been, and I physically feel ill that I've pushed her away, but I know it's what I need to do.

I turn away because I know that's the only way I'm going to be able to walk out of here right now. "I'll see you, Angel."

"My name is Brooke."

With the door open, I look at her. "I know your name... but you're my Angel."

And with that, I leave. I can't wait for the elevator. I go to the end of the hall and all but run to the stairway. I need to put some distance between us before I do something stupid... like take from her exactly what I want.

# Chapter 3

## *Brooke*

A week. Almost a whole week goes by, and he still hasn't talked to me. The night he left, I barely slept at all. All I could think about was that kiss. I wanted more, but it was like he couldn't wait to get away from me. I just don't get it. I thought the kiss was good. Heck with that – it was the best. At least for me it was. But obviously he didn't feel the same.

I've done my best to put him out of my head, but everything makes me think of him. I see a man with longer hair, I think of Lane. I see a man with a beard and I remember the way the stubble on his chin scratched my face when he kissed me. I see a man with tattoos and it makes me wonder about the ones I haven't seen on Lane but I know he has. Everything makes me think of him.

The next day and every day since I've seen him. He's still following me. I saw him at the grocery store, outside my yoga class, and my work. I thought he would come up to me, say hi or something, but he didn't. As soon as I would notice him, he seemed to disappear in the shadows. Almost to the point where I was beginning to wonder if I imagined seeing him.

By Friday night, I've had enough. My friends are going to the club on Saturday, but I didn't want to wait another day, and I didn't want any distractions from my plan. So here I am, back at Blaze and alone this time.

I'm watching him and see the first time he notices me. He's shocked but seems to recover quickly. He stares at me from across the room, and I wait for him to acknowledge me with a nod, a wave, anything. But I get nothing except for a heated look. Even from where I'm sitting I can feel how much he wants me. *So why is he acting as if he doesn't?*

"Do you want to dance?"

I drag my gaze from Lane and up at the man standing next to my chair. He's tall, handsome, and dressed impeccably. "What?" I ask him over the music.

"Do you want to dance?" he asks me.

I stare up at him and admittedly if I had met him a few weeks ago, prior to Lane, I would probably say yes. But now, I can't even look at him without comparing him to my gruff but gentle stalker. Unable to resist, I look at Lane. He's staring a hole in me, and the demanding look he's giving me makes my spine tremble. He wants me. He may not want to admit it for some reason, but he wants me.

"Sorry. I can't. I'm waiting on someone," I tell the man apologetically. At least I didn't lie. I am waiting on a man; however, it's more like I'm waiting on him to come to his senses than anything else.

The guy shrugs. "Maybe another time."

I don't give him a yes or no, just a smile before he turns and walks away. I can physically see Lane relax as the man walks away from me, but he still doesn't come my way.

I go and dance... and he watches me.

I order a drink and take sips, savoring the flavor as it hits my tongue... and he watches me. His eyes never leave me, and just knowing that has my panties soaked and me squirming in my seat.

I order another drink – a shot for courage. And as soon as the bartender sets down the short glass of tequila, I down in it one shot. The liquid burns going down my throat, and I suck air as if that's going to cool it. Taking a deep breath, I stand up and march toward Lane. He may not want to talk to me, but I want to talk to him.

I should be nervous. I'm not the type of girl that goes after a man. But this is different. I've had a taste of him, and now I want more. I'm fed up with the cat-and-mouse game we seem to be playing, and it seems he wants to follow me around but that's it.

I stop right in front of him, the toes of my strappy heels almost on top of his black boots. I put my hands to my hips and cock my hip out. I have all the confidence in the world at work and in the courtroom, but here, in the bar with my plus-size curves, I have to fake it to make it.

"Thank you for helping me last week," I tell him.

He points to his ear, letting me know he can't hear me. I grip the soft T-shirt material of his black shirt and scrunch it between my fingers, bringing him down closer to me so I can talk into his ear. "I said, thank you for helping me last week."

He's nodding as he turns his head to speak into my ear. "How's your hand?"

"Good," I tell him. He nods again but doesn't say anything else. He pulls back, looking at me expectantly.

The only thing that eggs me on is the way his heart is beating rapidly under my palm and his nostrils are flared. When I figure out that he's not going to ask me out or say anything for that matter, I take it into my own hands.

"Will you go out with me?"

He's about to say yes. I can see the interest in his eyes, but just as quickly he tamps it down. "I can't. I have to work."

That wasn't the answer I was hoping for. I rear back from him a little, and my feet get tangled underneath me. I almost fall to my ass, but at the last minute, Lane is leaning over me and holding me to him. Our faces are mere inches apart, and he's staring at me longingly. The music is thumping around us, and flashes of light are dancing across the room, but he's looking so deep into my eyes I can't look away. Someone bumps into me, and he puts one arm out to block the guy and other one tightens around me in a protective hold, pulling me against his hard chest.

"Do... you get a break?" I ask him breathlessly. And then, realizing he probably can't hear me, I pull him in close. My lips graze the curve of his ear, and his body shudders against mine. "How about a break? Do you get one of them tonight?"

He nods.

I unwind myself from his arms and point to my seat I had just left. "Great. I'll wait. I want to talk to you on your break." And before he can answer, I walk away, finally releasing the breath that I didn't know I was holding.

I sit with my legs crossed and watch him. Week after week he watched me, and now it's my turn. I'm not shy about it, or blush and look away like I have in the past. No, this time, I'm watching him like I own him, like he's already mine.

He works the crowd but never seems to go far. No matter where he's at, he always looks back at me like he's worried that I'll disappear. I do my best to keep my eyes on his face, but that's hard to do. He has a body that men are jealous of and women want. He's strong and confident with an air of cockiness that pulls people in.

I slide my thighs together and know that my panties are soaked he's that damn fine. He walks past me, and his eyes are on me the whole time. I can't look away, and when he walks by I stare at the way his jeans hug his ass. He walks by the next table, and a drunk woman leans out of her chair and pinches Lane's ass. Instantly, I'm pissed. Who the hell does that woman think she is? Jealousy burns inside me, and my first instinct is to give the woman a piece of my mind.

But I sit while rage builds inside me. I'm giving the evil eye to the woman, but it's obvious she's three sheets to the wind and doesn't have a clue what she's doing. Lane makes his rounds across the room, but it isn't long before he starts walking back my way. I want to watch him, but the drunk woman next to me is loud and giggly as she gets excited about his approach. I can already guess what she's going to do before it happens, and right then and there I decide it's not going to happen – not on my watch. When Lane gets close, he watches me curiously as I stand up, smoothing my skirt down my thighs. I move to the edge, and when he gets close, the woman hoots and hollers, leaning out to him.

I step in front of her. "Don't touch what's not yours," I tell her in the snootiest voice I can muster.

The woman laughs, but her friends must know that I'm not joking around or the fact that Lane is standing at my back, his hands on my shoulders, because they pull the woman back into her chair. I can hear Lane behind me say, "I'm going on break." And I assume he's talking to the other bouncers, but I'm not going to take my eyes off the she-devil, not when she's this close.

Lane pulls me with him and hustles me across the room. He doesn't say anything, and his grip is tight on my hand. Tugging me into an office, he shuts the door and pushes me against it. "What are you doing?"

Well, shit. He looks mad. Is it because he didn't want me to interfere? Maybe he wanted that woman to touch him. "What do you mean, what am I doing?"

He leans down real close until I can feel his hot breath on my cheek. "I mean you've been sitting on that stool watching me, every move I make. You almost got into a fight with some drunk chick."

I shrug my shoulders. "She shouldn't have grabbed you," I tell him.

"And... and you've been sliding your legs together like you need the friction, as if you're imagining me between those sweet thighs." He leans in and takes a deep breath. "Fuck, Angel. I can smell you. Is that for me?"

I don't even give in to the embarrassment I should feel. Yeah, it's for him. I've never wanted someone so much in all my life. But I don't answer his questions. I ask my own. "How long have you watched me? I saw you outside my apartment building, outside my work and at the gym. You follow me all the time... but you act like you don't want me." I slide my hands up his chest and curl my fingers into his shirt. "My question is... how many times have you stroked your cock thinking of me?"

# Chapter 4

## *Lane*

I drop my head and rest my forehead on hers. Hearing cock from her sexy lips is going to be my undoing. I've done all I can to stay away from her. Yes, following her, watching her is an addiction. But I could have kept doing that and only that. Until she touched me. Now I know I need more. Watching her is not going to be enough.

"Yes, I watched you. Because I couldn't not watch you. You're like a drug to me," I admit to her and wait for disgust or even fear to cross her face. I wait for her to pull away from me and run from the room. But she doesn't. Her face brightens, and she slides her hands around my neck.

Her lips touch mine, and I forget to breathe. I've dreamed of this moment a thousand times, and it's here. I don't want to scare her, but my hands tighten at her waist, not trusting myself not to deepen the kiss even though that's exactly what I want to do.

"I like it when you watch me. Do you want to watch me now?" she asks me softly, her chest rising and falling in little pants. I know I must be mistaken, she's not going to undress here, but then she starts to do exactly that. She starts at the buttons on her shirt. Slowly, she undoes each one, and by the time she's at the last one, my cock is hard and lengthening in my pants.

She pulls the silky material from her body before tossing it to a chair. Her black bra is lacy and barely contains her large breasts. She reaches behind her, and it's then I realize I'm standing here with my mouth hanging open. I slam it shut, and she pauses.

"Do you want me to stop?"

My throat is thick, and I don't think I can manage the words, so I shake my head side to side. *Keep going*, my head is screaming. I don't want her to stop until I'm pounding so deep inside her that I don't know where I end and she begins.

She undoes her bra, and her large, heavy breasts spill from the silky material. Instantly I reach for her, cupping her, running my fingers over her taut, rosy nipples. She gasps but arches her back, pressing her breasts firmly into my hands.

She unzips the back of her skirt and lets the material fall down her legs. She picks it up, just to toss it with her shirt, and I can't take my eyes off her. I've imagined this a thousand times, but even my imagination has not done her justice.

She's got curves. Fuck, my balls clench painfully, does she have curves. I gaze at her up and down, and the longer I stand here, the more I want her. Because I can't stop myself, I grip her hips, loving the feel of the silky material of her panties but knowing I need them gone. "Off." I grunt at her, putting my fingers into each side of her panties and pulling them down her legs. I fall to my knees, and her creamy pussy is right in front of me. She's standing, naked, with only a pair of heels on her feet and pearls around her neck. I inhale deeply, knowing she's already wet for me. She wants this.

She's staring at me, and I can tell she's wondering what I'm going to do next. With my hands on her hips, I grip her tightly. "Spread your legs."

I wait to see how she's going to react to my demands, but she makes me proud when she opens her legs to me. Her hands go to my shoulders, and as I move in, my face nuzzling her most secret place, she grips on to me tightly.

I run my tongue through her wet, swollen slit. She groans, going on her tiptoes like she's trying to get away, but she doesn't realize it. She's offered herself to me, and I'm taking it. I'm going to make sure she never forgets this.

The taste of her on my tongue makes my whole body quiver in need. I raise one of her legs and lift it over my shoulder, giving me better access. I go straight for her clit because I want to please her, and I want her to come undone in my arms. I want her begging for mercy. I wrap my lips around her clit. The sound of the back of her head hitting the door as she tosses it back vibrates around the room. Her hands have moved to my head, her fingers threading through my hair as she holds me to her and moves her hips in circles. I pleasure her like my life depends on it. Any time she pleases herself, I want her to wish it was me instead. I want to be the touch she needs, the one she craves.

She comes with her leg wrapped around my neck like a vise. She floods my face, and I lap it up, reveling in the taste of her.

I lift her leg and set it to the ground. Rising from the floor, I kiss my way up her body. My cock aches, and there's nothing on this earth that is going to please me more than getting inside her tight snatch.

I cup her chin tenderly, forcing her to look at me. Her eyes are heavy, but she looks satisfied. "I need to be inside you."

"Yes," she moans.

I pull her up into my arms, and she groans. "I'm too heavy."

Suckling her neck, I reluctantly pull away. I won't let her say shit like that. "No. You're perfect."

I walk with her across the room and set her on the edge of the desk. Instantly, her legs part, and she's like a fuckin' wet dream, legs open, her pussy glistening from her recent climax. With the taste of her on my lips, I unbutton my jeans and yank down my zipper. I'm hard. So hard for her.

I pull down my pants to my knees, wishing I'd taken the time to remove my shoes, but it's too late for that. I'm going to come soon, and I want it to be inside her, bareback so I can feel her tighten all around me.

"Oh God!" she whispers loudly as she draws her knees together.

No way. Fuck that. I push in between her legs to hold them open. I stroke my hand up and then down my hard length. "It's going to fit. That pussy was made just for me, Angel, and I need it."

---

Brooke

He's big. Too big. It's probably going to hurt, but I don't care. There's no way I can get up and walk out of this room until I've had him inside me. I reach for him, wanting to touch his soft, velvet length, but he jerks his hips from me.

"No. Not now. I'll come in your hand and that's not what I want. I want inside you, filling your womb."

His words are dirty and explicit, but I'm not surprised. I knew that sex with Lane wouldn't be like anything I've ever felt before. "I'm on the pill and I'm clean."

"I'm clean. I'd never do anything to hurt you." He's cupping my face, looking at me like he's not going to continue until I believe what he's saying. What he doesn't understand is that I already know he wouldn't hurt me. I don't know how, but I do.

"I know," I tell him, pulling his face closer to mine. "I need you, Lane."

He reaches between us and strokes his length along my wet folds. With each brush of his cock along my clit, I lift my hips, wanting more. "You like that, Angel?"

"Yes," I moan as he does it again.

"Good. That's good," he says as he lines himself up and pushes slowly inside me. My insides are sucking him in, and when he pulls out slowly before thrusting back in, I'm overcome with all the emotion. Every bit of it.

I wrap my arms around his neck, wanting to be closer, and obviously he does too, because he lifts me up off the desk and continues thrusting inside me. Over and over, he pounds into me, and all I can do is take it. My whole body is on fire, and I can feel myself tautening again as another orgasm starts to peak. "I need you to come, Angel. Come for me."

And with his hard cock pummeling me, his deep voice commanding me, I come at the same time he explodes inside me.

"Yes. Fuck yeah," he grunts.

He holds me to him, both of us panting. My legs slide to the floor, but still he doesn't let me go. Only when I feel like I can stand on my own two feet does he finally release me. "Are you okay?" he asks as he pulls up his pants, tucking his cock inside before zipping up.

He grabs a tissue box off the shelf, and taking a few out, he bends down in front of me. I wave him away. "I got it."

He watches as I clean myself, and I swear he looks upset, which causes me to tense. I hand over the box. "Don't you want to clean up?" I gesture between his legs.

But he's already shaking his head side to side. "No, I want you on me," he tells me matter-of-factly. And even though it sounds filthy, it sends a thrill through me.

I nod and turn away from him so that I can get dressed. Now that it's over, I'm self-conscious. I can feel his eyes on me as I get dressed. He's probably looking at every dimple of my thighs, so I try to cover up as fast as I can. Once everything is covered, I turn to face him. "I better go."

"Yeah." He picks up his earpiece off the side of the desk and puts it in. "Hey, Mike, I need you to follow Angel home. Make sure she gets there safely."

I'm shaking my head. I don't even know who this Mike is. "I don't need someone to follow me home. I'm a big girl."

He shrugs his shoulders. "It's the way it has to be."

I could stand here and argue with him about it, but I know I'd be arguing for nothing. What I want to do is ask him if this is it. Is this all he wanted? Am I out of his system now? It's on the tip of my tongue, but pride stops me from saying it out loud. If he wanted more, maybe to take me out, surely he would ask me.

"Uh, okay, so I guess I should go."

He nods, and his lips are pulled into a firm line. He's holding back even now, and I don't understand. He doesn't look happy.

I go to open the door, wondering if he's really just going to let me leave, when he says my name. Well, the name he seems to have given me.

"Angel."

I turn so quickly it's obvious he has me on a string. "Yeah?"

"Are you okay?"

I do my best to smile. "I'm good."

He nods, and when he doesn't say anything else, I walk away. There's a man that has the club's name across his shirt, and he nods at me. This must be Mike. I don't have the energy to talk him out of following me. I just continue on as if my life just didn't just get flipped and turned upside down.

# Chapter 5

## *Lane*

I just let her walk away. I didn't even try to stop her, and I know it's going to be the biggest regret of my life. This has all gotten out of hand. I never meant to touch her, let alone have her. Before I would have been able to control my urges, but not now.

The rest of the night, I stand in the corner of the club, my arms across my chest. I get a text from Mike. "Angel is secure."

That message should make me rest easier, but it doesn't. Before it would have, but now all it does is make me wish I was with her, and that I was the one that took her home.

If only we weren't worlds apart. She graduated in the top two percent of her class. She's a Wilson and an up-and-coming attorney. And even though she doesn't flaunt her family's name, it's obvious how much she's out of my league. Even though I've imagined a future with her, that's all it can be, and the sooner I come to believe it the better off I'll be.

Hours later, instead of going home, I drive to the high-rise apartments she lives in. I get out of my truck and climb onto the tailgate. Leaning back on my arms, I have a perfect view of her window. Just like the other nights I've come here after work, her light is off. And just like all the other times, I imagine her in her bed. But this time, it's more. I can not only recall what she looks like, I can remember exactly how she felt when she was in my arms. The little moans that she let out as I pleasured her have replayed in my head all night. Yeah, I'll never be able to go back to before. She's imprinted herself on me, and even if I wanted to, I wouldn't be able to forget her.

I sit until the early hours of the morning, and I know the doorman is about to change shifts before I pull out of the parking lot. Tonight is Saturday, and my hopes lift that I'll get to see her again if she comes in with her girlfriends.

---

## Brooke

He let me walk away. I've replayed the other night over and over in my head, and I know he wanted it—heck, he enjoyed it just as much as I did. But he let me leave.

The next morning, I went to yoga and the grocery store. The feeling that I'm being watched is overwhelming, but every time I look around, I never see him.

I skipped out on my friends on Saturday. By that point, I was second-guessing everything. I'm not the type to have sex in a bar, but maybe Lane doesn't know that. I pretty much pushed myself on him, and maybe if he had asked for my number or when he was going to see me again, it would be different. But he didn't.

By the time Monday comes around, I feel like I'm on edge and am going crazy. I have a lunch meeting with another attorney at the Gardens. It's a high-end sushi restaurant, and even though I hadn't eaten breakfast, I still am unable to eat. I know I'm being watched. I knew it this morning when I left my apartment, I knew it when I got to work and walked in the office building. The hairs on the nape of neck are not lying to me. Lane Davis is somewhere close. My body senses it.

During the lunch meeting, I look all around, ignoring Mr. Teller. "Are you okay?" he asks me.

Deciding that I can't focus on anything at this point, I tell him honestly, "Actually, I'm afraid I'm out of sorts today. I think we have gone through everything that you need for Friday's case. I'm going to take today and tomorrow to get it all prepared, and I'll bring it by your office tomorrow afternoon if that's okay with you."

"That's perfect. I'm impressed already with all you've found, Ms. Wilson. You are already proving to be an asset to the company."

I nod. "Thank you."

He gathers his belongings and picks up the check from the table. "Can I give you a ride back to the office?"

But I'm already shaking my head. "No. Thank you, though. I'm going to visit the ladies' room, and then I think I'm going to get some air and walk back to the office."

We part ways, and I walk down the hall to the bathroom, but instead of going in, I keep going straight until I walk out the back door of the restaurant and into the alley.

With my hands on my hips, I pace back and forth. There are busy roads at each end of the alley, cars and people walking by. But the alley is empty. This can turn out to be a very bad decision on my part, but I'm not thinking so.

I don't know how much time goes by, but I'm just about to give up. Maybe I'm wrong. Maybe Lane wasn't here and wasn't watching me. Maybe I'm going mad.

Just as I'm about to walk down the alley, the back door of the restaurant flings open, and a breathless Lane comes running out. He stops suddenly, and I note the look of relief on his face. I was right. He's here... and he's been watching me.

"Are you following me?"

He nods without answering, his nostrils flaring. It reminds me of the other night when he had the same determined look on his face; however, then he was pleasuring me, pounding in and out of me.

I cross my arms over my chest. I'm tired of this game. "Why are you following me?"

Pain is etched on his face. "I can't help myself."

I shake my head and put my hands on my hips, needing an explanation, so I ask him point blank, "Do you want to date me?"

"No," he says instantly.

Anger fills me. I was right. He wanted one night and got that from me. But that doesn't explain why he's following me. "Then what do you want?" I throw my hands up in the air.

# Chapter 6

## *Lane*

"I want you." I take two steps toward her, but then I take one step back. Even being this close to her is too tempting.

I know I should leave, but the look on her face makes me stand my ground. She deserves an answer, and I won't be anything but honest with her. "A date won't suffice. It won't even whet my appetite for you. I want you all the time. I want you in my arms. I want to wake up to you in the morning. I want to be the one you call when you need something – anything. I want to hold your hand. I want your perfect lips wrapped around my dick. I want your eyes on me and only me. I don't want any man to look at you, and if he does, I don't want there to be any doubt that you belong to me." I've given up on holding back. The more I talk, the darker her eyes get, and it's the same look she gave me when we were having sex the other night. I take one step, then another, and I don't stop until her back hits the brick wall. I press my body to hers, and fuck it feels like home. "I want you wet... for me."

I lean my head against hers. I'm weak. I should have stayed away, but I couldn't. There are people walking at the end of the alley. A car horn sounds, but all I can do is look into her eyes.

She's biting on to her lower lip, and it's driving me crazy. I reach my hand up and soothe her lip with my thumb. She opens her mouth and nips at my finger as I inhale sharply. "Fuck, give me a taste, Angel. Just one taste."

"Touch me," she says, her voice laced with lust.

"No one sees you. No one but me."

Her hands go up my chest and curl around the collar of my shirt. She pulls me toward her, and I go willingly. Our kiss is frantic. My leg is between her thighs, and she's grinding herself on me. I lift my knee, her feet coming off the ground, and she gasps.

"Don't let them, but I need you to touch me," she begs.

I shield her body as much as I can. She deserves so much more than to come in the alley, but she should never have to beg for anything. Whatever she wants, I'm going to give it to her.

I pull her skirt up enough so that I can slide my hand between her thighs. Her panties are soaked, and I pull them to the side, swiping my fingers through her heat. She moans and then puts her mouth against my shoulder and bites down. I flinch at the pain, but it doesn't stop me; if anything, it pushes me further. I stroke her, focusing on the bundle of nerves that is vibrating under my fingers. She's hot, horny, and ready. It doesn't take long before she's coming undone in my arms. I don't even wait for her to come down before I'm sliding her skirt back down her thighs. I've done my best to shield her, but if someone sees her, I would hate to have to kill them.

Because I'm a dirty fuck, I lift my fingers to my lips and lick them clean. When I have her taste on my tongue, I can't resist. I lean in and kiss her, shoving my tongue into her mouth, but she doesn't care. If anything, it just turns her on more.

---

### Brooke

We're in an alley in downtown Wilson. Any and everyone can walk by and know it's me in the alley, but I can't seem to make myself care. The way Lane's kissing me doesn't allow me to think of anything except him.

I pull away from his magical lips and stare up at him. He has to be the most handsome man I've ever seen... and he wants me. There's no denying it.

"I want..."

But before I can finish, he's cupping my face in his massive hands and looking deep into my eyes. "What do you want? Whatever it is, I'll make it happen."

And finally, after weeks of being on edge and unsure of the future, I feel like a weight has been lifted from my shoulders. "I want this," I tell him. "I want you to watch me. I want you to touch me and make me yours. I want to taste myself on your lips – that was hot, Lane." I run my hands through the stubble of his beard. "I want to feel your beard between my thighs, your arms around me. I want it all... with you."

Hope flares in his face, but just as quickly as it was there, it goes away. Agony is clear in his voice. "We're different. I'm different. Look at me and then look at you. No one is going to accept us. Not your family or your friends."

"None of that matters. I don't want you to be anything but you. It's you that I want."

He still shakes his head. "Your family..."

"Will love you," I tell him honestly. "My family may have money, but they're not snobs. As long as you make me happy, they won't care."

But he still is not believing me. "You don't even know me."

I loop my arms around his neck. I can feel him trying to emotionally pull away from me, and I'm not going to let him. I relay everything I know about him. The good and the bad. "Your name is Lane Davis. You're thirty-two. You had one parking ticket a few years ago, and you paid it the day you got it. You've been married but are divorced. She cheated on you, and I hope you know that I'm nothing like that – I would never cheat on you." He squeezes me tighter as if the thought makes him ill. But I don't let that stop me. I want him to know that I know it all. "You want to be a cop. You applied once at the local precinct but pulled your application before the decisions were going to be made. I just don't know why you withdrew. You were who they were going to choose, by the way. You are all about doing the right thing. I've seen you make sure drunk women make it home safely in Ubers. I've seen you pick up dropped money and return it to the rightful owner. You are protective of me. You like me, even though you act like you don't want to admit it. And well, to be quite honest, you're a stalker, but that doesn't matter to me as long as I'm the only one you stalk."

He blows out a deep breath, no doubt surprised by everything I know about him. "Ha, and you think I'm the stalker."

I just shrug my shoulders. Maybe we stalked each other. It doesn't matter now. As long as we end up together, none of that matters.

"It sounds like you about know it all."

I nod. "Yeah, except why you pulled your application, but you don't have to tell me if you don't want to."

He almost looks embarrassed. "You know Mike at work?" I nod my head, remembering the man that he had follow me home the other night. "His wife was sick, and I knew Blaze would fire him for missing so much work. I stuck around so I could cover his shifts for him."

I shake my head. I had no idea this man could be even better than I thought. How can he doubt he's good enough for me? "How's his wife?"

He looks surprised that I asked. "She's good. She actually just finished treatment, and they got all the cancer."

I pat him on the chest, trying to hold back the tears. "You're a good man, Lane Davis."

He doesn't look like he agrees with me, but at least he doesn't argue. Instead, he surprises me with a request. "Can I take you home?"

My forehead creases. "Are you going to stay with me?"

He nods, sliding his hand down my arm until he laces our fingers together. "If you'll let me."

We start to walk down the alley, but I stop, jerking him to a halt. "No turning back, Lane. You're mine now, right?"

He nods, leaning in to kiss my forehead. He whispers, "And you're mine, Angel."

# Epilogue

## Brooke

### Three Months Later

Today's the big day. My first big court case.

All in all, it's been a good day. I woke up to Lane between my thighs before he made me breakfast. We went our separate ways when he left for training for his new job as a policeman for the city of Wilson and I went into work. Right before I left the office, a huge bouquet of flowers was delivered to me with a note from Lane wishing me luck.

And now here I am, delivering the closing arguments for the case that I know I'm going to win. I've spent more than enough time preparing for this, and I know it in and out. I wanted this win a lot, and I worked my ass off for it.

As I finish my closing arguments, I walk back to my seat. The hairs at the nape of my neck stand up and I smile, sensing Lane's presence before I even see him. I lift my eyes, a smile already on my lips when I gaze out to the back of the room. But my smile drops when I spot him. He's sitting in the back row right next to my parents. I wouldn't even recognize him if he wasn't giving me the sweet smirk he's giving me now. I look him up and down, and I feel like I've been hit right in the chest. He has on a button-down shirt with a coat and tie, and his hair is styled, slicked back off his face. I frown and sit in my seat.

The jury finds the defendant guilty without even needing to take time to review the case. It all happens suddenly, and before I know it, I have colleagues surrounding me and patting me on the back. My client hugs me, and the whole time, my eyes are on Lane. When it all dies down, I walk right up to Lane and my parents. My mom is hugging him, and at least that calms me a little. He was worried about my parents not liking him for nothing. They love him. They're able to see what a great guy he is.

"Thank you all for coming. Are we still going to the restaurant to celebrate?" I ask the three of them.

"We sure are. You did great up there, honey." My father wraps me in a big bear hug, and I let him and my mom know that we'll meet them there. I'm smiling, trying to act like everything is okay, but it's not. As soon as they walk off, I turn to Lane. "We need to talk."

I don't wait for a response. I turn on my heel and lead the way out the back of the courtroom, down the hall and into a room where I know we can talk privately.

He walks in right after me, and he's smiling proudly at me. But after one look at my face, his smile drops. "What is it? What's wrong?"

---

Lane

My stomach is in knots. The instant she spotted me in the courtroom I knew there was something up. "Yeah, you don't look like someone that just won their first case. You look pissed."

"What are you doing?" she demands with a huff under her breath. She looks me up and down, and I guess that even though I tried to clean up a little for her, I probably shouldn't have come.

"You mean why am I here? Because I love you and I'm proud of you," I tell her.

"Yeah, well, I love you and I'm proud of you," she says, walking toward me. I can tell she's still mad, but she seems to be softening. I still don't have a clue what's wrong with her, but she told me she loves me so it can't be that bad. "But what I mean is, why do you look like that?"

I shake my head, still not understanding.

"A suit and tie. You've changed everything about how you look."

"I had to shave for work, you know that. And I didn't think you'd want me in here looking like one of the clients you have to defend with all my tattoos blaring for the world to see. I didn't want to embarrass you."

She rolls her eyes. She pushes the jacket off my shoulders and tosses it to a chair. Undoing my tie, she jerks it from my neck. "Of all the stupid..." She starts ranting at me, but I can barely pay attention while she's touching me. She unbuttons the sleeves of my shirt and rolls them up my forearms. Lastly, she undoes the top few buttons of my shirt and kisses my chest. "I love you, Lane Davis. You! Exactly the way you are."

I put my arms around her and cup her ass, drawing her in to me. "I love you too." I breathe her in. "I'm so proud of you."

She shakes her head. "You helped me a lot."

I start to shake my head, but she stops me. "Yes, you did. You helped me do research and listened to me when I needed to vent." She runs her hand up and down my chest. "You were always there when I needed to unwind and destress."

I know exactly what she's talking about. She's had a busy few weeks, and I made it my mission to give her an orgasm every day. I wish I could say I'm a good guy, but the truth is I'm a selfish prick. I wanted her. My need for her has only grown, and if I was able to relieve her stress by satisfying my need... well, let's just say I'm a lucky man.

"Yeah, well, I say we celebrate," I tell her and then remember her parents. "After lunch, I'm taking you home, Angel. I want to show you how proud I am of you."

Her body trembles against me, and she kisses my lips. "I hope I can wait."

She grabs on to my hand to lead me out the door, but I pull her to a stop. I'm not a romantic, and I'm probably going to screw this up, but I can't go another minute.

When she looks at me expectantly, I pull a small box from my pocket and drop to one knee in front of her. "I've been carrying this around since I met you. I need you..."

Her eyes are wide, and a look of shock comes on her face. Her hands tighten on my shoulders. "You have me."

I grip on to her hips and stare into her eyes. "No, I need you with my last name. I need your belly filled with our babies... I need it all."

She laughs, and I know she wants the same. "Ask me, Lane. Ask me."

"Will you marry me, Angel?"

She looks at me skeptically. "If I say yes, are you going to quit stalking me?"

I shake my head. "You don't have to worry about that. I'm always going to stalk you, sweet girl."

She takes the ring from me and holds it in her hand. When she can't take her eyes off me, I realize she doesn't care about the ring. It's me that she wants. "Yes, I'll marry you."

I swing her up into my arms and set down in the chair with her in my lap. I pull the box from her hands and take the ring out to show her. "I hope you like it. If you don't, we can pick out something else."

She holds her hand out, and I slide it on her finger. The princess cut diamond looks perfect on her hand. "I love it!" she says, looking between it and me. Her arms go around my neck, and she holds me tight. "I'm never letting you go, Lane."

My throat is thick with emotion. I may have followed her everywhere, but she's proven that she loves and wants me just as much. We may have met and fallen in love under unusual circumstances, but there's nothing or no one that can tell me we aren't meant to be.

"Give me some, baby. I just need a taste, then we'll go."

She does exactly as I ask. She leans in to me and seals her mouth to mine, and just like any other time she kisses me, once is not enough. Her family may be waiting a while.

## THE END

# Stalk Her Hard

Filthy Dirty Desires

Hope Ford

# Chapter 1

## *Sara*

I'm pushing his hand. I know I am.

But something has to be done. We definitely can't continue like this.

I started working at Tate Marketing exactly three weeks ago, and since then, my world has been turned upside down. It's not the job. I love the job. It's challenging, and as a junior marketing executive, I'm learning so much.

No, what has completely messed me up is the fact that I'm being stalked... by my boss.

It's been like this since day one. The day I came and interviewed for the job with Mr. Tate. I was hired on the spot. I'm good at what I do. I create ad copy and ad campaigns that sell. I've definitely proven myself in the short amount of time that I've been here, but I've learned that it might be possible that Mr. Tate hired me for other reasons.

I knew when I interviewed there was some chemistry. I felt it for sure. I knew it was a bad idea to accept the job, but he made it to where there was no way I could have turned it down. The pay he started me at is high, and I don't know any entry level marketing position that pays what he pays me.

When I accepted, I planned to just suck it up. I could work with him and let my little annoying crush dwindle away. Surely, he'd end up being an ass that yells or he'd be arrogant and ruthless. But it didn't work out that way. If anything, he's patient and ethical. He goes out of his way to help his employees, and he's fair. Which makes me want him even more.

On the second day on the job, I started getting texts from him. Completely inappropriate texts, but I didn't care. He told me he liked my skirt, and I wore one just like it, but shorter, the next day. He told me he liked my hair down, and it hasn't been up since. It's not been anything too out of the way, but each and every text holds the promise for more.

And then I felt him watching me. Anywhere I went, there was someone following me, but no matter how hard I looked, I never saw anyone. At one point, I was scared. It must have literally been on my face because I got a text from Mr. Tate.

"Don't be scared. It's me."

I remember looking at my phone, wide-eyed. Mr. Tate was following me.

I remember going home and drawing the shades to my apartment over my parents' garage. I was nervous, knowing that a man—a much older man— was following me. But the more I thought about it, the more excited I got. So excited that I started to enjoy it and play with him a little. I went to an "R" rated movie and watched it. I know he was there, but he never showed his face to me. When I got home that night, he sent me texts, innocent at first, asking me what I liked about it. But then the texts got bolder. He told me what he wanted to do to me, how he wanted to bend me over his desk and make me his.

So it became a game. I looked for ways to tantalize him, and he continued to flirt on text and secretly stalk me. But at work, it was like there was nothing between us. When we were face to face, it was like he was looking at a stranger. I couldn't read anything in his eyes when all I could think about was his fantasy, of bending over his desk and letting him have me.

So here we are. I've ignored all his texts today at work, leaving them unread. It's killing me to know what he's saying, but I'm determined to push his hand. One way or another, this is going to end.

"You look beautiful, where are you off to?"

I look at my coworker Christy. She's been a good friend to me since I started here. She's patiently taught me all the ins and outs of everything. I smile at her and try to seem excited. "I have a date."

Her face brightens. "Ooooh, a date? That's so exciting. With who? Where are you going?"

I'm loud as I answer her even though I don't really think I need to be. It seems that Mr. Tate knows everything already, but I do it anyway. "It's a guy I went to college with. He's asked me out a few times, and I finally agreed. It's time for me to start dating."

Christy sits on the edge of my desk. "And where are you going?"

"Just to dinner. We're going to try out that new Italian restaurant that opened up down the street last week."

Christy snaps her fingers. "Antonio's? You'll have to let us know how the food is and we can all go to lunch there one day."

I grab my purse out of my drawer and put it over my shoulder. I have on my black leather skirt. I hemmed it last night, and it's now two inches shorter from the last time I wore it. My shirt is a thin material that cuts low on my chest. I'm showing way too much thigh and too much cleavage, but right now, I don't care. "I'll tell you all about it tomorrow. See you in the morning."

I wave bye to her and to a few of my other coworkers that are still here. I don't even have to look up at the $2^{nd}$ level; I can feel Mr. Tate's eyes on me. But the ding of my phone in my purse is a dead giveaway. I almost reach for it, but I don't. I step outside of the building and take a deep breath. I'm glad I told Ronald to meet me at the restaurant. I need to get myself together.

I take my time walking down the street. My phone rings, and I reach in my purse to grab it. Mr. Tate has

never called me, but when I look at the caller ID, I
see it's him. I hit decline on the call and keep
walking.

I figure he'll call back, but he doesn't. *Quit thinking
about him*, I tell myself.

I drop my phone in my purse and cut the corner just
a few feet from Antonio's, and there stands Mr. Tate,
leaning against the brick wall. He straightens as I get
near. I look at him and then the door to the
restaurant. I can ignore him, but I remind myself that
he is still my boss.

I stop when he steps in my path. "Mr. Tate."

His jaw is set, and I swear I can hear his heart
beating in his chest. "Don't do this, Sara."

I look up at him innocently. "Do what?"

He points at the door of the restaurant. "This."

I blink as if I'm clueless. "What? Go on a date?"

His jaw tightens even more, making me worried he's
going to break something in his mouth or something.
"Yes. Don't go on this date."

I jut my chin at him. He's mad. I can see that he's livid, and it makes me wish I'd never made these stupid plans. But then I remember why I did it. I can't continue on like this. If he wants me, he's going to have to make a move. "It's too late to cancel. I'm doing it."

I step around him and get a foot past him when his hand goes to my wrist. He stops me and leans down to whisper into my ear, "If he touches you, I'll kill him."

I gasp and look up at him. I start to laugh and suck it in, slamming my mouth shut. He's not joking. He's completely serious. The look he's giving me is lethal. I gulp and nod my head.

He releases me, and with one backward glance at him, I walk away.

Fuck, what have I gotten myself into?

# Chapter 2

## *Daniel*

Her skirt is too short. That's what I've been thinking about. She's not comfortable in it. She yanked at it all day long. I've gotten nothing done today because I've had to give Thomas, an employee, a list of things to do to keep his eyes off Sara. It's obvious he has a crush on her, and it will be over my dead body before he acts on it.

So I've kept one eye on Sara and the other on Thomas... all fuckin' day.

I've tried to figure out why she would wear a short skirt like that, and now I know. As she goes in to go on a date with another man, I have it all figured out. She's trying to make me jealous. I guess we're past trying because I'm way past jealous. I'm ready to kill a mother fucker just for looking at her too long.

I count to ten and then walk in the door behind her. I spot her across the dining room sitting across from some schmuck I've never seen before.

I tip the host a twenty to get seated close to Sara and her date. As I sit down, right in her line of sight, I can't help but think about how this is all new to me. Usually when I stalk her, I make sure she doesn't see me. Oh, she knows I'm around; I can tell by the way she fidgets and looks around for me. But this time, I'm leaving no room for error because I'm sitting right at the table next to them. For the first time, I want her to know exactly where I'm at, and I don't want her second-guessing if I was being honest about killing the asshole drooling over her. I'll kill him in an instant and not even think about it.

Since the moment I laid eyes on Sara, she's been mine. What started as texting has moved to a whole other level. I've stalked her. That's the only way to put it. I've literally kept track of her every move, even installing listening devices at her desk so I could hear her voice during the day. The only time I can't see her is when she's in her apartment over her parents' garage, but even then I sit outside, parked on the busy street and just watch, waiting for a glimpse of her.

I'm staring a hole in her, and she's uncomfortable, but I can't make myself care. Eventually the man that is sitting in front of her with his back to me turns to see what she's staring at. I look at the man, or I should say boy. He looks as if he's probably still in college. I glare at him, and his eyes get big and he turns back around. *That's right, dickhead, I'm right here. All I have to do is reach over and I could snap your skinny neck without even getting out of breath.*

She's trying to explain who I am, and I watch as she stutters over the words. She doesn't know it yet, but I'm her man. She may have thought this little game of going out with someone else was okay—well, it's not. There's nothing okay with another man thinking he may have a chance with what's mine.

They don't even order dinner. They each order dessert and coffee, and the punk eats faster than I've ever seen anyone eat in my life. As soon as the waitress brings the ticket, the man throws some bills on the table. They get up to leave, and the guy reaches in like he's going to hug her. My girl freezes up just as I growl. He must hear me because he stops moving with his arms midair, and then he drops them to his sides.

He turns and looks at me, and I raise up from my seat, standing to my full height. I know he's not challenging me. Fuck it. I have some energy to wear off, and nothing would make me happier than putting a fist in that college boy face of his. I take a step toward him, and he bolts, running out the door. And even though I'm glad he's gone, it pisses me off too. I could be a dangerous man for all he knows, and he's left her here alone with me. He's definitely not worthy of her.

Sara is glaring daggers at me. I reach in my pocket and toss a hundred dollar bill on the table before walking over to her. She doesn't wait for me; she turns on her high heel and stalks out of the restaurant. I follow her at a slower pace, watching her as she storms away from me. Men and women alike all watch her. She's beautiful and seems to draw attention wherever she goes. She walks the few blocks, picking up the pace the closer we get to the office. Her anger must fuel her because I have to move faster to keep up with her.

When we get to the parking lot at the office, I lean against the brick wall as she unlocks her car door. She raises her head and looks at me. Yep, she's still mad. Even from here, I can tell she's pissed. I can't really blame her. I know I just ruined her night.

She stomps toward me, and I suck in a breath.

"Stop stalking me. Stop texting me. Just stop."

I shake my head side to side. "I can't."

"You're driving me crazy."

I nod, because I understand where she's coming from. She's driving me crazy.

She throws her hands up in the air and turns to go. I should let her go and cool off, but I can't keep it to myself any longer. "You're mine, Sara Chambers."

She turns so fast she wobbles on her high heels. She steadies herself and stares at me. She thinks I'm crazy. I can see it by the way she's staring at me. "How? Because you stalk me and send me texts? I'm not yours, Mr. Tate. You're going to have to try a little harder if you want me to be yours."

I simply nod at her. She gives me another dirty look and walks back to her car. I stay where I'm at, my arms crossed over my chest.

She wants more, I'll give her more. "Challenge accepted."

# Chapter 3

## *Sara*

I barely walk in the door at the marketing firm the next morning when I hear a beep from my phone in my purse. I walk across the office, nodding at my coworkers as I go by. When I get to my desk in the corner, I drop my bag in my seat. Reaching into my purse, I pull out my phone and open the text message: "Nice skirt. Did you wear that for me?"

My head raises instantly, and I look all around. I didn't even have to look at the caller ID to know who the text is from.

I get one similar to this every day, multiple times a day. When I don't spot the man I'm looking for, I look to the open second floor to see if I can see him looking at me. Goosebumps have already formed on my arms, which is a good indication that his eyes are on me. But I've learned that even though I may not see him, he definitely is watching me.

What started as just flirty banter has gone to a whole new level recently, and after last night, there's no doubt he's stepping up his game.

First I was uncomfortable with the attention my boss was giving me, but I can no longer fight it. Even though none of my coworkers have a clue, Mr. Tate has an obsession, and that obsession is me. I jerk as the phone in my hand dings again, and I look down and read the text message: "Answer me. Did you wear that skirt for me?"

The professional side of me knows that I should answer him by telling him no. And admonish him for his unprofessional question. But I can't. I'm still mad at him, and I thought about it the whole night. And it was after pondering on the whole situation that I discovered my problem. I'm on edge completely because I'm sexually frustrated.

I grimace and look at my phone. I type in one word, in all its honesty: "Yes." My eyes are glued to the phone as the little bubble show up, letting me know that he's about to respond. It's like I can't breathe, waiting to see what he has to say.

And when I see his response, I suck in a breath. "Good girl," it says. A smile forms on my face, and I look around the office again, trying to spot Mr. Tate. Even though I'm mad, I still seek his approval. I mean, those two words, *good girl*, have my heart racing and my panties getting wet. I know he's watching me. He's always watching. It may have made me nervous before, but now it is my complete undoing. No matter where I am or when it is, I can always feel his eyes on me. It's like an ongoing sexual foreplay that keeps my panties wet and my body primed for more.

He's stalking me. I know he is, but he's yet to touch me besides that slight touch of my wrist last night.

But I want more. My body craves him. And I know that it is forbidden. He's the last person I should be interested in. He's off limits. He's my boss.

My phone dings again. "You're rubbing your thighs together. You need more, don't you, baby?"

A soft whimper escapes me, and I bite my lip to stop it. He has me completely on edge, but I think he knows it, and I think that's how he wants it. I wasn't lying when I told him he was making me crazy.

"Sara, can I get you a coffee?" I know I look guilty as I shake my head at Christy. She's standing at her desk that is right next to mine. She's been nice to me since I've come to work here, and she's looking at me curiously. "Are you okay?" she asks.

I know my face is heated and my eyes are wide as I stare back at her. "Yes, I'm... I'm fine. No, I don't think I need any caffeine today. Thank you, though."

She stares at me a second longer. "Is everything okay? How did your date go?"

A part of me wants to spill the truth about Mr. Tate and put all my burdens on the table. I don't have anyone to talk about what's been happening, and I know it would be helpful to have another woman's perspective. But I don't dare. I can't risk losing my job. I give her my best smile, hoping to hide the worry and lack of sleep that is probably evident on my face. "Yes, I'm perfect. But my date... well, I don't think I'll be seeing him again. He was nice, just not for me."

She nods. "Don't worry. You'll find someone when you least expect it." She lifts her cup at me and walks over to the kitchen area. I watch her to make sure that she doesn't look back at me before looking around the office again.

That's when I see Mr. Tate. He's come out of the shadows. He's standing on the second floor, his arms flexed as he holds on to the banister in front of him. He's leaning over, staring at me, and he doesn't seem to be worried at all about being caught watching me. I stare up at him, and his look intensifies. Even from here, I can see the desire in his eyes.

I want to harness the anger I felt for him last night, but seeing him watching me hungrily, the anger fades away. I can't stay mad at him, not when he looks at me as if I hung the moon and the stars.

I cross my ankles and tighten my thighs together. I ignore the pull in my lower belly and stare back at him. The look he's giving me says it as plain as day. If I doubted his attraction to me before, there's no mistaking it now. He wants me, and I don't think he's going to stop until he has me. My only question is for how long and will I be able to survive it when it's over?

# Chapter 4

## *Daniel*

I made sure there would be distance between us when she spotted me. If I was on the first floor, close to her, there would be nothing stopping me. The need to have her is intense. Even more so now. After the little stunt she pulled last night, I know it's almost time. She's all I think about. She consumes every thought I have, and this obsession is getting out of hand. She's nothing like any woman I've met before.

What started off as something simple turned into this complex, fierce desire that I can no longer tamp down. Even from here, I can see how her breathing changes as she stares back at me. I know I need to walk away, break the gaze that we have on each other so that no one sees, but I can't. I watch as her breath hitches and her shirt seems to tighten across her breasts as she arches her back a little. And the way her eyes seem to go to a dark green instead of her normal, bright green. All of it is a dead giveaway that she wants me just as badly. She thinks she's kept herself guarded, but I see every thought she has. Her eyes give it all away.

She juts her chin at me as if she's daring me to come down there to where she is. My girl is getting impatient, and I can't say that I blame her. I clench the banister in front of me, shake my head and force myself to move back to where our gaze is no longer connected. I walk off without another backwards glance and slam the door to my office as I walk through it. I'm rock hard, but that's nothing new. I've been like this since the first day, when she came in her little black skirt to interview for the position.

She knows I like that skirt, and that's why she wore it today. I didn't have to ask her; I already knew. But I wanted her to know that I know.

I move and sit behind my desk. I try to focus on the projects at hand, but like always, my thoughts go back to Sara. I open my side desk drawer and turn on the listening device that I have. When I first installed it, I felt a little shame, but not anymore. It's not like I'm trying to catch her in anything. All I want to do is hear her sweet voice.

I've learned a lot about the people that work for me from listening, but it's nothing I would use against anyone. But most importantly, I've learned about Sara. She's a hard worker that chips in on any project. She's calm, has to think things through, and is very dedicated to what she is doing. She never participates in office gossip. And when her coworkers complain about the hours I demand of them, she doesn't join in. Her work ethic makes her even more desirable, if possible.

It's noon when I hear them talking about going out to eat. I listen as they discuss where they're going, standing over my desk staring at the speaker. My heart starts to race in my chest, preparing for the chase. The thought of her being out in the world, away from me, is too much for me to bear.

I'm never invited for these lunches; none of the higher-ups are. Funnily enough, though, I go to every one of them now. But I'm never seen. I always sit far enough away to keep an eye on Sara. And today is not going to be any different.

As soon as I hear the group leave, I'm on the move. I'm well known in this city and am a patron at all the restaurants downtown. I've learned how to discreetly enter and exit a restaurant, using back doors most the time.

I settle myself in the back corner and listen.

I know the instant she senses me here. She seems to always know when I'm around. She always rubs her hand up and down her arms and then looks around as if she's looking for me. A tiny frown forms on her face when she doesn't find me, and that makes me smile.

Sara orders a salad. I want to order her a real meal. Just from listening in at work, I've heard her talk about needing to lose weight, which is not true. Her body is perfect just the way she is. I don't want her to change a thing.

She sips on her water as her coworkers all talk around her. I notice Thomas making eyes at her, and it's obvious that he's interested. It makes me want to fire him to get him as far away from her as possible.

Obviously, all the extra work yesterday didn't get my point across. I'll have to fix that.

I haven't staked my claim yet, but as soon as I do, he'll know then that she's off limits. As I sit here and listen to Thomas flirt with her, I'm thinking of all the crap jobs I'm going to give him when he gets back to the office. He's going to be too busy to worry about flirting after today.

I've built this company from the ground up. I've always been completely focused on my business and making it what it is today. And I've never let anything get me sidetracked, except now. Sara has me turned upside down, and it seems like everything is off kilter. But as soon as I make her mine, that's going to fix it all. Nothing else matters. Nothing at all.

# Chapter 5

## *Sara*

"What do you say, Sara? You want to go out for dinner one night?" I stare back at Thomas, knowing he expects an answer. The truth is I'm not even the least bit interested in him. Maybe before I met Mr. Tate, Thomas would've been the kind of guy I would want to go out with, but not now.

I look around at the faces of my coworkers. I can see the surprised look on Christy's face like she can't believe he just asked me out in front of everyone. Truth is I can't believe it either. It's not like I've ever encouraged him or led him to believe I'm interested, but I know I need to let him down easy.

I give him an apologetic look. "I'm pretty sure that there are rules against dating coworkers." Thomas shrugs his shoulders like it's not a big deal. As if Mr. Tate would just overlook it. But he doesn't know Mr. Tate like I do. I know Mr. Tate is not going to go for it.

Luckily, I'm saved from any further explanation when Christy says, "I'd quit my job if Mr. Tate wanted to date me." Christy, it seems, has always had a crush on Mr. Tate. From what I hear in the office gossip, he's never dated anyone that has worked here, so this jealousy that I feel is unfounded. I can't really blame Christy for being attracted to him.

The conversation continues, but luckily it moves on to other things, and Thomas drops the subject of us going out with each other. Everyone eats, and before it's time to be back, I hear a ding from my phone in my purse. I don't even have to look at it to know it's him. I haven't seen him, but I know he's here. I can feel his gaze on me even right now. As everyone is turning their credit cards in to pay for their meals, I pull my phone out and nonchalantly look at the text. "Tell them to go on without you. You'll be along in a minute."

My heart starts to race in my chest. Is this it? Is this the moment that I've been waiting for? Is he finally going to touch me? I clench my thighs together in anticipation, and when the server brings back our check cards and we all sign our bills, we get up, knowing that we have to get back to work soon. We're on our way toward the door, with me lagging behind, when I tell them, "Hey, I see someone over there I know. I'll be along in a minute."

Thomas stops while the rest of them go ahead. "I can wait for you."

I shake my head. "No, there's no reason for you to be late getting back too. Please go ahead. I'll be there soon."

He looks as if he's going to argue with me, but finally he turns and walks out the door. I look around the restaurant, waiting for Mr. Tate to appear.

My phone dings, and I read it. "Go to the ladies room."

I turn quickly and walk toward the back of the restaurant. I open the door and look at the stalls, waiting on him to step out. After opening the door to each one, I find they're empty. I'm the only one here.

I stare at my phone and wait for the next instructions. But I'm surprised by what it says next: "Thomas likes you." I don't even try to deny it. Mr. Tate watches me, and I'm sure he has seen the way Thomas flirts with me.

Another text appears. "Do you like Thomas watching you, flirting with you?"

I type in my response. "I like you watching me."

Even though there's no way he has his eyes on me now in this little space of a bathroom, it's like I can feel his approval anyway.

His text comes in quick. "Good girl."

Those two words shoot straight to my heart. I don't know what it is, but I like knowing that I pleased him. I don't even know this woman that I've become. I should be telling him off, not listening to his orders or seeking his appreciation. But I've also never felt anything like this before. I've never wanted a man like I want Mr. Tate.

Before I can ask him why I'm standing in an empty bathroom, the bubbles appear, letting me know that he's sending me another text. "I left you something. Check the inside pocket of your purse."

I pull my purse off my shoulder and set it on the counter, almost frantically searching, I unzip the pocket and reach in, pulling out the foreign object. I stare at it with my mouth hanging open. First of all, I have no idea how he put this in here. My purse is almost always with me. Well, except when it's in my drawer at the office and I attend a meeting or go to the ladies' room.

I take out the little silicone object and hold it in the palm of my hand. I've seen these before, but I've never owned one. I know exactly what it is. It's meant to bring pleasure, and I can't believe that my boss just gave me a wearable clitoral vibrator.

My phone dings, and I almost drop the sex toy. I grab it in one hand and hold on to it firmly as I look at my phone. The text has me taking a deep breath. Just three words but it's enough to make my whole body start to shake with adrenaline. I gulp and read it again. "Put it on."

"Holy fuck," I mutter. Surely, he doesn't expect me to... what, put this on and just leave it there all day?

I can't. And I'm about to tell him exactly that when he sends me another text. "Be a good girl, Sara. Put it on. I wanna play."

Shit! Just his words in black and white on the screen of my phone have my panties wet. I don't even have to touch myself to know that I'm soaked. There's an ache in my lower belly, and a part of me wants to know what happens next.

But do I dare? I look at myself in the mirror and stare back at myself judgmentally. I'll die if anyone finds out.

There are so many questions, but I'm not going to ask him. I'll play his game... for now anyway.

# Chapter 6

## *Daniel*

She's mad. I can tell by the way that she stalks out of the restaurant that she is mad. I'm an asshole too because I like having her all fired up. After telling her to put it in, I got a response from her that said, "Now what?"

But I know she didn't like my answer because all I told her was, "I'll see you back at the office."

I stand in the alley and watch as she walks across the street, back toward our office. She's mad, and her eyes are like daggers as she stares all around, trying to find me. I stay hidden, though, because I know that I need this game to last a little longer. I need her to want me as much as I want her, and she's not there yet. She's not even close.

I wait five minutes after she walks into the office before I sneak in the back door and head up to my office. I turn the recorder on so I can hear her at her desk. It's normal day-to-day happenings. People are busy answering phones, talking, working. I pull the remote out of my pocket and stare at it. There are ten levels of intensity on it. I turn it on and hit the up button to turn it up to one level. I hear her gasp across the speaker of the listening device.

I guess I took her by surprise.

I smile, knowing this is going to be good. I stand up and go to the window that overlooks the first floor. If I stand to a certain side, I can see her, but she can't see me, and I watch as I turn the remote up to level two.

She jumps in her seat, and I see her smile over at Christy as if Christy asked her if she was okay. She has a smile frozen on her face as she looks all around the office, searching for me. I turn the remote up to level three, and her head falls back on the chair, her mouth forming a perfect "o." She's so responsive. It makes me imagine what it's going to be like whenever I'm balls deep inside of her.

I reach down and adjust my hard cock.

She lifts her head, letting me know that she's over the first initial shock and trying to pull herself together. I try to imagine how wet she is right now. I would love to jack off and watch her come at the same time, but I can't do that to her. Plus, I don't want anyone to see her come. No one but me.

Instantly, I turn it up to a level four and watch as her hands clutch on to the armrest of her chair.

I could do this all day, watch the pleasure on her face. But unfortunately, I don't have that option. I have a meeting that I cannot get out of, but I'm not ready for this to be over. I watch as a few of the senior ad executives walk up the stairs toward the boardroom. They're all going to be waiting for me soon.

I hit the power button on the remote and put it in my pocket. I walk back over to my desk, hitting intercom on my phone. It rings down to Sara, and I can hear the surprise in her voice when she answers it. "Yes, Mr. Tate?"

My voice is thick, and I grunt at her, "There's a marketing meeting. I would like for you to come and attend." I put emphasis on the word come. No one else will make anything of it, but I'm sure she will.

She's silent for two seconds before she asks me her question, and I can hear the hesitancy in her voice. "Do I need anything?"

"Just yourself," I answer, and I disconnect before I say something that I know I shouldn't be saying. No doubt the rest of the office is listening to our conversation. I go back to the window and watch as she gets up. She walks as if tiptoeing away from her desk and then she walks back to it, grabbing a pad of paper and a pen off the desk.

She clutches the pad to her chest, and I imagine she's covering the erect nipples pressed against her blouse. She walks slowly up the stairs, and I walk out of my office and meet her at the top.

I want to reach out and put my hand at the small of her back and lead her back to my office instead of a boardroom full of other men and women. Embarrassingly enough, I'd only need five minutes alone with her, and I'd be burying my seed deep in her womb. She does that to me. I'm like a ticking time bomb where she's concerned.

But I know I can't do that. I put my hands behind my back and hold them there. "Thank you for joining us," I tell her.

She blushes prettily and blinks her long lashes at me. Right before we get to the door, I open it, and as she walks past me, she looks up at me, her eyes wide with innocence. "Anything for you, Mr. Tate."

My grip on the door tightens, and I stand there and watch as she walks into the room. Fuck, she's asking for it.

If anybody is surprised to see her join in on the meeting, no one lets on. But it's not like anyone is going to question what I do anyway.

She takes a seat at the opposite end of the room from where I'll be standing. She's trying to look professional as if she didn't just make an obscene promise to me. Anything for me... the sound of her saying those words keeps replaying in my head, and it goes straight to my dick. She doesn't have a clue who she's playing with, but I plan on showing her.

# Chapter 7

## *Sara*

I sit in the back corner of the room and try to be as low-key as I can. Everyone is looking in the opposite direction. They're all looking at Mr. Tate, but it feels like Mr. Tate has eyes only for me. He's talking about the new contract that we have with a cell phone company. There's discussions of the target market for the phone and where the marketing dollars should be spent, and they briefly touch on ad copy and different campaigns they plan on running.

I take notes because I assume that's what I'm here for. I've never been asked to one of these meetings before, so I try I to soak it all in and learn something even though all I can do is think about Mr. Tate. I didn't have time to remove the vibrator. I cross my legs and try to be focused on the task at hand.

Mr. Tate is standing at the front of the room with his hands in his pockets. "What about you, Christopher? How do you think we should focus our ad campaign?" He's looking at Christopher, which is across the room from me, but all of a sudden I feel the vibrator tremor right against my clit. It feels like it went to the highest level it's been on, and my body convulses as it shakes against my already sensitive clit. I almost break the pen in my hand as I clench around it. My whole body is pulled tight, and I know I'm close to having an orgasm, but just as suddenly, the vibration stops, and Mr. Tate turns to look at me.

"What about you, Sara? I know this is your first time joining us, but do you have an opinion?"

I blink at him, feeling as if I'm coming out of a complete daze. I didn't even hear Christopher's answer. I say the first thing that comes into my head: "Sex."

The laughter and snickers from my coworkers sound around the room, but Mr. Tate looks at me, and his jaw tightens. "Excuse me?"

Thankfully, he's turned off the sex toy, and I'm starting to come back to my senses. I shrug as if my outburst was not a big deal. I know my face is red and flushed, but I continue on as if I didn't just scream sex to a crowded room. "As we all know, sex is what sells. What about this phone is different than others? This one has location software on it. It has listening software. That's one angle that we can take. A little friendly, romantic stalking."

There's a buzz around the room as everyone starts to talk at once. I see some of them nodding their head in approval and some others shaking their heads in displeasure. But the only one whose opinion matters to me is staring at me as if he is fighting a temptation. He pulls at the collar of his shirt as if to say it's hot in here.

When Mr. Tate doesn't say anything, everyone starts to quiet down, and they turn their attention to him. He's staring at me with the most molten look he's ever given me. It's like I know what he's thinking, and it has everything to do with the sex toy between my legs.

People start to look between Mr. Tate and me with curious expressions. He's about to give it all away, so

I blurt out the first thing I can think of. "What do you think, Mr. Tate? Bad idea? Maybe the wrong demographic."

He seems to jerk out of the trance he was in and looks around the room. "It could be a good angle." He looks at Christopher. "Do some research on it, please."

Christopher nods and looks at me with a smile. He raises his pen in the air to get the boss's attention. "Do you want Sara to work on this with me?"

Mr. Tate's whole face tautens. He levels Christopher with an angry glare. "No, I don't."

Christopher seems taken aback but recovers quickly. "Sure, okay."

The conversation continues as others call out ideas. For the rest of the meeting, I keep my head down and take notes. Thankfully, Mr. Tate doesn't mess with the remote control in his pocket anymore.

It seems shortly after my outburst the meeting is over. I grab my pen and paper, ready to make a run for it, when Mr. Tate's voice rings above everyone else's. "Sara, can you stay back for a minute please?"

He points to the table to the seat directly across from him. "Have a seat."

Everyone turns and looks at me, and by the apologetic faces, they probably think he's going to get on to me about my outburst. That's fine with me. I'd rather them think that than what's really happening here.

I let everyone pass me by as I walk back over and sit down in the seat across from him. As the last person shuts the door, he pulls the remote control out of his pocket and sets it down on the table in front of him.

"I liked your suggestion," he says.

I nod, not trusting my voice.

He leans forward, resting his elbows on the table. He's rolled the sleeves of his dress shirt up, and I can't seem to take my eyes off his strong forearms. "Are you okay?"

I drag my eyes off his arms and to his face. That's a loaded question if I've ever heard one. There's a part of me that wants to say to hell with this, strip down to where I'm naked and ask him to take me. He's enjoyed watching me go to the brink and then drawing me back in. No doubt he likes the control.

My whole body feels as if it's on fire and I'm going to erupt at any point. I can't take it much longer. This is madness. There's a part of me that hates him for putting me through it. I need to come. I need it now. I lean forward, and his eyes drop to my exposed cleavage. "What do you think? How the fuck do you think I am?"

# Chapter 8

## *Daniel*

Her lower lip is puckered out as if she's pouting at me. I know I've probably gone too far. If nothing else, the curse words leaving her mouth is enough proof.

She reaches across the table as if she's going to grab the remote control, but before she can, I wrap my hand around it and pull it back toward me. I stare into her eyes. "You realize that blurting the word sex in a room full of men, that's what they're going to think of now when they look at you."

She crosses her arms over her chest and leans back in her chair. "I don't see how you could think that is my fault."

I lean forward. "I don't want anyone looking at you and thinking about sex. No one but me."

She shrugs her shoulders. "That's not my problem."

I grit my teeth and stare back at her. The need to lay her back on this big table and cover her body with mine is overwhelming. I could take her right now, and I know she wouldn't stop me. The way she looks at me she wouldn't say no. But I have plans for her.

I lean back in my chair and raise my hand with the remote in it. Her eyes flash from my hand back to my eyes. Just as her forehead creases, I turn up the remote to level one, and she grips the side of the table.

With my eyes on her, I push the button to take it up another level. And then another. Her eyes close.

I lean forward and grunt the words at her. "Open your eyes and look at me."

As I say it, she pries her eyes open and glares back at me. She could stop this at any point. She knows that she can, but she doesn't want to. She just sits there and takes it.

I hit the button to take it up another level, and her body jerks.

She shifts back and forth in her seat, riding the toy that has her clit fully engorged. I turn it up another level, and this time she moans loudly into the room.

She's close. I know she's close... and I turn the toy off.

She reaches her hand across the table, and I pull the remote control out of her reach. I control her pleasure. Just me.

She's glaring at me with daggers in her eyes. "No, I need to come, Mr. Tate."

I jut my chin at her. I want to hear her call me by my name. "Daniel," I insist.

Her body shakes as if she's shivering. "I need to come, Daniel." It comes out like she's begging me to give her the release that she needs, and I don't have the heart to deny her. I would give anything to have her come on my dick right now, but there's a time and a place for everything.

I turn the remote control up to a level one. "You need to come, baby?"

She whimpers and bites on to her lower lip, nodding her head. I turn it up level by level until I get to the ninth notch on the remote. Her body starts to convulse. As the orgasm shoots through her, her lower hips are shifting front to back, over and over as if she's riding the chair she's sitting in. Her face is pulled tight from the immense pleasure. She groans and moans over and over because I don't turn the toy off. I let it continue bringing her to another orgasm. "Argh!" she bellows.

All my life, I've never watched anything as beautiful as her coming. I turn the machine off, and it's like she falls forward onto the desk, her arms splayed out, her head lying softly, and she's panting as if she's just run a mile. I count to ten trying to get myself somewhat under control.

I want my hands on her, but I know once they are there, we've reached the next level.

"Are you okay?" I ask her softly.

She raises her head and is glaring at me. She stands up and teeters on her feet. She grabs on to the back of the chair to steady herself. She lifts her tight skirt up her thighs and then reaches between her legs. She pulls the toy out and lays it on the table in front of her. It's slick and covered in her juices.

She's mad, really mad. She walks away, but before she gets to the door, I bolt to it and stop in front of her. I grab her hand, the one that she had just had between her legs, and I pull it up between us. The cream from her body is glistening on her finger and I can't even try to stop myself. I pull her hand to my face and suck her fingers into my mouth, licking her clean. She's staring at me, watching me taste her. I moan around her fingers. She's like the sweetest honey. But it's not nearly enough. I won't be satisfied until I have her completely.

When my lips pop off her fingers, I kiss her knuckles.

She tries to appear bored, but I can read her like a book. Her question surprises me, though. "Why are you doing this?"

It has to be obvious. "Because I want you."

She shakes her head. "What? You want to fuck me... what do you want... I don't understand."

I put my hand on her chin and force her to look at me. "You're going to be mine... fuck that, you're already mine."

She almost looks bewildered, staring back at me. "If you want me... why would you not just ask me out on a date? I don't understand any of this."

I lean down until our mouths are just a fraction of an inch away from each other. "You're a special woman, Sara. I knew it the first time I met you. You're not someone a man can ask out and just hope they say yes. My way...you're going to know and feel exactly how obsessed I am with you. You're all I think about, and when I claim you..."

She whimpers and urges me to continue. "Yeah?"

I cup her jaw and whisper, "When I finally claim you, sweet Sara, you will be mine and only mine. I'll never share you."

I know better than to kiss her, but when she moves her head and presses her lips to mine, I suck in a breath because the real thing is better than I've ever imagined. I kiss her as if my life depends on it. Her hands go around my neck, and she moves against me. One leg lifts, and she hooks it around my hip. My cock is hard, and I thrust my hip against her, wanting her to feel just how hard she makes me.

I could pick her up and carry her to the table and make her mine right now. But I don't.

I kiss her one more time, savoring the feel of her lips on mine, and then I pull back and set her away from me.

Her eyes are large in her face, and her lips are swollen. "Why'd you stop?"

I press my hand to her belly. "Because when I make love to you, I'm going to want it all, Sara. And I'm not going to take it on a table here at work."

She shakes her head. "But..."

I smooth the hair that is sticking up on her head. She's going to be mad at me now, but I'll make it up to her later. I release her and step back. "Thanks for coming."

She looks at me in disbelief. Her mouth falls open, and then she huffs and walks out the door. I lick my lips because I know that soon she's going to be mine.

# Chapter 9

## *Sara*

I barely get to my desk and Christy walks toward me with a worried expression on her face. "Are you okay?" she asks.

My hand instantly goes to my hair. Oh my God, she knows, and if she knows, everyone in the office knows. "I... uh..." I start to stutter.

She pulls me in for a hug and then leans back to look at me sympathetically. "I heard about the meeting and your little, uh, outburst."

I let out a big whoosh of air. Oh, thank God! "Uh, yeah, Daniel... Mr. Tate caught me off guard and..."

She's shaking her head. "I know. It was your first time at the meeting and you got tongue-tied. Trust me, I get it. Don't let what they say bother you."

I look around the room. What does she mean *what they say*? I start to question her when I hear someone across the room scream out, "Sex!" And then another person the opposite direction does the same. I look both ways and then at Christy. She's still patting my shoulder, trying to soothe me. "It's okay... they'll get over it. Just ignore them."

But Christy is wrong... terribly wrong. My little sex outburst in the meeting has turned into the office joke. All afternoon I've had to listen to people laughing about it. It's been a roller coaster of a day, and my emotions have been all over the place. Even though my and Mr. Tate's relationship, if that's what you want to call it, has gone to a different level, it's not enough.

I still want him. I'm probably a fool, and he's probably going to break my heart, but I have felt his eyes on me all afternoon. It's almost closing time when Thomas walks over to my desk. "We're all thinking about going out and getting a drink. Do you want to join us?"

I look at him and try to appear disappointed. Shaking my head, I tell him, "I'm sorry. I can't. I have plans already."

He nods. "Sure, sure. Maybe some other time."

I nod but don't comment. I know it's stupid, but I don't think Mr. Tate would appreciate me going out for drinks with Thomas. After the stunt he pulled this afternoon, I shouldn't care, but I do.

I wait for everyone to leave, until it's only Mr. Tate and me left in the building. I think about pushing the button on the intercom and letting him know that I'm leaving, but I stop myself. There's no point. I've learned that no matter what, he knows where I am at all times. I'm not sure how, but he does.

I put my purse over my shoulder, push my seat back in, and then walk across the office, the sound of my heels clip-clopping across the hardwood floor. I walk out of the building without a backward glance. Instead of going to the parking lot and to my car, I walk across the street and then cut down an alley. It's already starting to get dark, and our office is located downtown. I know better than to just walk by myself like this, but there's no part of me that is scared. And it's all because of Mr. Tate. Without even seeing him,

I know that he is close on my heels. I know he won't let anything happen to me.

I turn down another alley, this one darker than the one before. But I don't slow my step, I just keep moving.

When I get to the back entrance of a popular bar, I walk in and head straight to a vacant table. I order an Old Fashioned from the waitress, and then look around the room. The bar is full of people stopping in to get a drink after work. I spot some of my coworkers, and before I can look away, Thomas sees me and starts walking over to me.

He sits down without even asking. He takes a swig from his beer bottle. "You decided to come."

I shake my head. "I'm supposed to be meeting someone... a friend," I explain. It's a lie. I'm not meeting anyone, but I do know that Mr. Tate will be here before long.

Thomas nods his head, not the least bit turned off. "You mind if I keep you company while you're waiting?"

I should tell him that yes, I do mind. I know that Mr. Tate is not going to be happy, me sitting here with another man. But a part of me is still mad at him. "Sure. I would love for you to stay."

That seems to get him excited, and he sits up a little straighter in his seat. "What can I get you to drink? A beer?" He snaps his fingers. "A shot of tequila?" he asks.

But I point at the approaching waitress. "I've already got my drink."

"Thank you," I say to the woman as she lays down a small square napkin on the table in front of me and then sets the drink on top of it.

She nods. "Sure thing, honey. And it's already been paid for."

I nod, not the least bit surprised. I take a small drink of the Old Fashioned and let the whiskey and the smooth orange taste travel down my throat. The goosebumps appear on my arms again, alerting me that Mr. Tate is close by. I look around the bar, but I'm not holding my breath. There are way too many places here for Mr. Tate to stay hidden.

Unless....

It's like I can feel Mr. Tate's heavy gaze on me, and I know he's mad. I'm picturing his nose flared and a grim look on his face as I smile at Thomas sitting across from me. I want Mr. Tate to be jealous. After the torture he put me through today, I need this, whatever this is, to be taken to the next level.

He may have thought that since he gave me an orgasm, that I should be happy, but that's not how that works. I won't be happy until I have Mr. Tate between my thighs, and he's burying himself inside me.

I look around the bar, hoping to get a glance of Mr. Tate. But I don't. I know he's here, though. Thomas says something, I'm not for sure what it is, but he laughs afterwards. I take my punishment a little further and put my hand on Thomas' arm and laugh with him.

Not two minutes go by and the same waitress comes to me. "Ms. Chambers?"

I'm not even surprised when she says my name. "That's me," I say.

She looks at Thomas and then back at me. "Your meeting is being held upstairs in a private room. He's waiting on you, he told me to let you know." I grab the Old Fashioned off the table.

"Thank you," I tell her. "And thank you for keeping me company, Thomas. I'll see you tomorrow at work."

I walk away and follow the waitress up the stairs. She points down a hallway. "It's the second door on your right."

I nod, ignoring the curious glance that she sends me. I try to calm my nerves as I walk down the hallway and stop at the second door. I count to three and push it open, knowing that what is on the other side is about to change me forever.

# Chapter 10

## *Daniel*

It's like I'm holding my breath until I see her walk in the door. She's in trouble for so many things. I think she knows it too. She walks in the door, shutting it behind her. Her one hand is in a fist at her side, and her other hand is holding a drink, no doubt an Old Fashioned. She brings the drink to her mouth and takes a sip as if she doesn't have a care in the world. She licks her lips and sets the drink on the table next to her before putting her hands on her hips. "You wanted to see me, Mr. Tate?"

I laugh. "I think we've reached the point where you can call me Daniel."

She takes a few steps into the room toward me and stops with only a few feet between us.

"Okay, Daniel, you wanted to see me?"

I laugh because how can I not? She knows that she holds all of the power here, knows that she's got me tied up in knots. I look at her in her eyes, daring her to look away. "Did I see you flirting with Thomas downstairs?"

She doesn't even blink. "You saw that, did you?"

I growl and take a step toward her. "You know I did. I see everything that you do."

She looks at me accusingly. "You stalk me."

I shrug my shoulders. I'm not going to deny it. "Yes, I do."

She shakes her head. "I don't like this game anymore."

I move toward her until our bodies are only inches apart. I can feel her breasts brush against me every time she inhales. "You didn't like this afternoon in the boardroom?"

She rolls her eyes. "You mean when you made me come?"

With one finger I brush a stray hair off her shoulder and then I lift my hand and let it rest on the base of her neck. "Are you telling me that you didn't like it?"

Her pulse is racing underneath my palm. "I liked it, but it wasn't enough."

I have to agree with her on that. I enjoyed watching her come undone, but I want more. "Tell me what you want."

She's like no woman I've ever met before. She says it exactly as it is, and she goes after what she wants. She leans her head back so she has to look up at me. "I want you to make me come. No toys. The only thing I want is you."

She surprises me when she reaches out and cups my hard manhood. I lean down and press my forehead against hers. "I'm mad at you right now."

Her hand tightens on my balls before releasing them and then moving up my shaft. "You don't seem like you're mad."

I grit my teeth. "You touched another man."

She seems to think about it for a minute, and her soft voice responds, "You mean when I touched Thomas' arm?"

"Yes, and he's lucky he didn't touch you. If he had, he would be in a gutter somewhere right now."

She smiles at me. "I knew you were watching. That's why I did it. I figured I owed you for the torture that you dished out to me earlier today."

"Torture? How did I torture you? I can still taste you on my tongue. There was no torture... only pleasure."

She wraps her hand around my girth through my pants and squeezes. "I don't want some toy to please me. I want this inside me."

My hips jerk. "Fuck," I moan. "I'm going to kiss you now," I tell her, and I don't wait for a response. I press my lips to hers, and it's like I'm home. That's the only way I know how to describe it. Our mouths mate, moving, discovering each other. I press my tongue to the seam of her lips, and she opens for me. Our tongues meet in a duel, and I swallow her moan as she lifts up on her tiptoes, pressing her hips into my groin.

I had so many plans for this. I wanted to draw it out, bring her to the edge and then back again. I wanted her the first time in my bed... our bed. I need her to want me, but there's no way I'm going to last. I'm going to come in my pants if it continues like this.

I pull back, panting. My hand goes around the base of her throat, forcing her to look at me. I search her eyes, and she's already so far gone just from a kiss. "You want to come."

She nods, even though I meant it as more of a statement than a question.

"There are rules... things you'll have to agree to before I bury my cock inside you and make you scream."

She whimpers in response.

"I will be the only man from here on out..."

Her eyes widen, and her cheeks turn a bright red. "You'll be my first..."

My hips buck, and my hold tightens on her. Her first... I'm going to be her first. "And your only."

I look at her as if challenging her to disagree. She rolls her eyes at me. "It's not like I sleep around or anything."

I want to spank her ass for her sassy mouth, but I don't. Right now, I can barely think straight.

She draws me back on the subject at hand. "What else? What other rules do you have?"

"I won't give up stalking you. I'm not wanting to control you, but I have this crazy desire to make sure you're safe and that you're protected." I hold my hands up in front of me. "I won't give in on this."

She lifts her shoulder in a shrug. "I like you following me."

I let out a breath I didn't know I was holding. "Okay."

Her eyes widen. "Okay? That's it? That's all the rules?"

There's a thousand other things I want to say to her to convince her that I can be enough for her, but I can't get the words out. I need her now, more than ever. "Let's get outta here."

She shakes her head. "No."

I'm not used to being told no and am temporarily shocked. "What do you mean, no?"

She slides her body against mine. Every curve fits against me perfectly. "It means we're not leaving. I'm done waiting. I want you now."

"I'm not going to let your first time be in some private room at a bar."

Her hand slides up my chest and stops when she gets to my pebbled nipple. Her finger draws circles around it. "Will you let anyone watch me? Watch us?"

I draw in a harsh breath. "No!"

"If someone came in, would you protect me? Block my body so no one would see me?"

I let out a severe curse. "Yes! No one would see you. I'd cut their eyeballs out if they did."

She blinks up at me. "And what if we do have sex... right here... and someone came in thinking they'd get a turn next..."

I don't even let her finish her sentence. "Fuck. That. I'd kill them. I wasn't lying or exaggerating, Sara. This isn't a game to me. You. Are. Mine! No one will ever touch you."

She pats my chest almost soothingly. "Okay."

I nod as she steps away from me, thinking we're going to leave now, but she surprises me. She pulls her shirt from the waistband of her skirt. Slowly, she pulls it over her head and lets it fall by our feet. For a second, I forget to breathe. "What are you doing?"

She shrugs as she shimmies her waist, pulling the skirt down over her hips. "You convinced me that I'll be safe... here with you."

"Always," I tell her.

She smiles indulgently. "You convinced me that I'll ALWAYS be safe with you. Well, I don't want to wait anymore. I want you... now."

"Sara..." I plead with her.

She stands up, wearing only a dainty pair of black panties and matching bra. She reaches behind her and unclasps her bra, letting the straps fall down her shoulders. She drops the bra and then puts her fingers in the side of her panties, shoving them down and letting them fall to her feet. She steps out of them, and I forget to breathe.

She smiles, knowing exactly what she's doing to me. "You okay?"

I swallow roughly. I'm losing all control here, and she knows it. "Yeah, I've never been better."

I grab her wrist and tug her toward me. She leans her body into mine and starts unbuttoning my shirt. I put my hand on hers to stop her, but she swats my hand away. "I want to feel your hard chest pressed against me."

I can't argue with that. I jerk my shirt open, buttons flying everywhere. I pull the material off and sling it to the floor. She's already pushing my white T-shirt up my body, and I pull it the rest of the way off. Her hands are all over my chest. I pull her flush against me, enjoying the feeling of her breasts pressed firmly against me.

I lean down, kissing down her neck and not stopping until I'm suckling her hardened nipple. Her hands are on my bare shoulders, and she's digging her nails into my skin. I suck in a breath at the pain she inflicts on me. It hurts... so good.

I slide a hand between us, stroking a long finger through her wet, swollen folds. She moans, rising on her tiptoes. My finger pumps in and out of her. "You're ready, aren't you, baby?"

She whimpers as I go a little deeper.

I know I have a mess in my pants. I can feel the sticky precum coating my shaft. I pull away from her, releasing her and stepping out of her reach.

Her eyes fly open. "No! Don't do this to me, Daniel. You say I'm yours... well you're mine, and that means when I want it... I get it."

The possessive tone of her voice has my hips thrusting forward. I'm so ready to be inside her. I pull up the chair behind me. I pull my pants and underwear down to my ankles and sit down in the chair. My erect cock is sticking straight up between us. I grab her hand in case she tries to get away. Not that I'd let her, but just in case. "You want it? Come and get it."

Her mouth falls open as she stares at my long, thick girth. With a lick of her lips, she drops, almost landing on her knees. I catch her and pull her up onto my lap. "You'll not kneel on this floor, Sara."

She looks surprised. "But I want to taste you."

I cup her jaw. "There will be plenty of time for that, but I made a promise to protect you, and you resting your bare knees on this dirty floor is not protecting you."

She starts to argue with me, but I stop her with a kiss. Just a quick one before pulling back and looking at her. "I told you that I'd protect you. There's no maybe or chances I'm going to take... If I think something might hurt you, it's not going to happen."

She reaches down between us and wraps her hand around me. "Even if..."

I shake my head. "Even for my pleasure. I'd love to have your mouth on me, but we have time for that. Tonight it's all about you."

She scoots up, straddling my lap. I put my hands on her bare ass and pull her to me. My cock rests between her opened thighs, her juices coating my shaft and balls. She's primed and ready as she settles against me. I'm so close. I'm not even inside her yet and I'm ready to shoot my load.

I reach between us, lifting her up and positioning my cock at her entrance. I draw it back and forth along the seam of her lips, coating her wetness along my shaft. Her hips shimmy and shake over top of me, and when she starts to slide down the length of me, I hold my breath. She's tight. So damn tight.

# Chapter 11

## *Sara*

For weeks I've imagined this. I've dreamed about being with Mr. Tate, or I guess I should call him Daniel since I'm sitting on his lap, his dick inching into me. I slide slowly down the length of him, his cock stretching me. This is so forbidden. Not only is he my boss, but he's older than me, and I know he should be off-limits, but I have no control when it comes to him.

I'm panting, almost afraid to take him completely. As I hover over him, he talks to me in a soft voice, urging me on. "I promise I'll make it good for you, Sara."

But I still don't move.

His hand moves to my cheek, bringing my face up to his. "Look at me."

I blink and look at him with wide eyes. "I..."

I'm about to tell him I can't do it, but he shakes his head. "Do you trust me?"

I nod instantly. How could I not trust him? He's protective and maybe a little overbearing, but he'd never hurt me.

His eyes drill into mine. "Say the words."

I let out a puff of air as I slide just a little lower. "Yes. I trust you."

He nods. "Good girl."

And that right there is my undoing. I slide the rest of the way down his length, pushing down so he breaks the barrier keeping us apart. I grunt at the flash of pain and hold myself tightly against him.

He searches my face. "You okay?"

I tilt my hips and rock a little. "Yeah... but I want to move."

He laughs, and I feel his tremors as he moves inside me. He grips on to my hips, lifts me up a little and then back down. I groan at the friction. I want to savor it, but already I'm so close. His hands grip on to my hips, and his fingers dig into my skin. I know I'm not the only one feeling this. The way he's staring back at me tells me that he's completely obsessed.

I start to move again. I lift up and slam back down onto him. He groans, his head falling backwards as I move my hips back and forth. Instead of a slow, steady build, it's immediate. It's like I've had foreplay for weeks now and I'm finally going to get to come, for real this time, with him inside me. He kisses me, my face, my neck, my shoulders. He massages me, rolling my peaked nipples between his thumb and forefinger, but all that does is turn me on even more. I lean back in his lap and put my hands on his knees behind me and rock into him.

He reaches down between us and puts his finger on my clit. Back and forth, he applies pressure, and it becomes too much too fast. The feel of him sliding in and out of me and the immense pressure on my clit takes over. My hips start to move uncontrollably. It's like I'm possessed as I rock back and forth on top of him, losing all control. I'm so close. So close.

His voice is like a growl in the dark room. "Come for me, Sara, come on my cock." And I do exactly as he tells me to. I come, and my whole body tightens as the orgasm rips through my body. He moans and groans, and I feel him swell inside me as he shoots his cum deep inside my womb. I take it all, milking his shaft until he's empty.

Completely spent, I throw myself forward and rest my head on his shoulder. His arms come around me, and he holds me tightly pressed against his hard chest. One hand is on my ass, the other is rubbing up and down my back. I can still feel the slight tremors and the twitches of his cock that is still inside me.

I thought the orgasm I had earlier in the boardroom was something. Damn, it was nothing compared to the earth-shattering pleasure I just received.

That's when it hits me. I just fucked my boss. I raise up and search his eyes, looking for some indication that this is more than just a fuck. I know he said all the right things earlier, but maybe it's normal for men to tell you what you want to hear in the throes of passion. He's looking at me, his forehead creased, but he doesn't say a word. Not a damn word. Surely he'd say something right now if he doesn't want me freaking out and running from the room.

I pull myself together and raise up. He slides out of me, and I pick my underwear up off the floor behind me. I almost lose my balance as I rise up from the floor. I get dressed, throwing everything on really quickly. I brush my hand through my hair and try to look everywhere but at Daniel... I mean, Mr. Tate. I almost slap my hand to my head. *What have I done?* I know that I look like I've just been thoroughly fucked. That's how I feel, anyway.

I turn to go because I don't know what else there is to say at this point. I hear him stand and soon after, the sound of him zipping his pants up. "Stop," he says.

I stop with my hand on the closed door. I should just open it and run out of here. But I don't. I don't turn toward him, though. "What do you want?"

"Don't you dare fucking walk out of here," he says.

I gasp and turn and look at him. "Don't talk to me like that."

Immediately he looks like he's sorry. He grabs the white T-shirt off the floor and puts it on and then grabs the shirt with all the missing buttons. He walks over to me and puts his hand under my chin and pulls my face up to where I have to look at him. "Sorry. I didn't want you to run out of here."

"We were done. I was going to go home."

He squats in front of me and lifts the hem of my skirt. My legs squeeze together. "Uh, what are you, uh doing?"

He looks up at me. "Remember, I said I'd always look out for you."

I nod.

He tries to pry my legs apart. "Open up."

I do as he says.

"Good girl."

I put my hands on his shoulders to steady myself as he raises my skirt up. I'm a little freaked out, but I stand here, legs wide open and watch him as he stares between my legs.

He raises the shirt in his hands and wipes it between my legs before folding it up. "You have some blood on your thighs."

I want the floor to open up. I reach for the now stained shirt. "Here... I'll take it."

He shakes his head, putting the shirt under his arm. "No, I'll take care of it."

The way he says it tells me he's not going to be getting rid of it or anything. I'm not sure I want to know what he's got planned for that shirt.

He fixes my skirt back and stands up, grabbing my hand. "I'll run you a bath at home."

I try to pull away. "I can take a shower at my apartment."

He grunts, "You're going home with me."

I look at him, surprised. "I am?"

He nods his head. "Yes. I'm not done with you yet."

Part of me is elated knowing that there's going to be more of what just happened. But another part of me knows that for my own sanity I can't continue this, not like this. Not knowing it can end in an instant.

"Yet?" I say to him.

He shakes his head. "I misspoke. I should have said ever. I'm not done with you ever. Will you please go home with me?"

So many questions are in my head, but I can't put a voice to any of them. I merely nod, and when he tries to open the door behind me, I put my hand on his chest.

"I need to go first. Your employees are down there, and I know you don't want them to see us like this. I'll meet you."

But he's already shaking his head, pulling the door all the way open. He leans down and pushes his lips to mine and pulls away with a grunt. "Maybe I haven't made this clear, Sara, but you're mine. I don't care who knows it. From this point forward, you are mine."

I put a hand to my chest, right over my heart. It's beating in triple time. "You were serious about that?"

He grabs on to my chin and hold me in place. "Yes, I was fuckin' serious about that. Anything that has to do with you, I'm serious about."

I take a deep breath. There are so many things we probably need to talk about, but none of that seems to matter right now. I stand up on my tiptoes and loop my arms around his neck. I push my body against his, fitting my curves against the hard muscles of his torso. "Take me home then."

He pulls me up, kissing me until I'm breathless. When he releases me, he doesn't let me go far. I'm tucked under his arm as we make our way down the stairs, and I swear I hear him whisper, "Good girl."

# Epilogue

## Sara

I think I lost him. I'm not sure, and I definitely wouldn't bet money on it or anything, but I'm pretty sure I lost him.

Daniel wasn't joking when he said he was going to continue stalking me. He's done it since the day he met me and every day since.

A part of me feels guilty right now because when he finds out I'm gone, he's going to not only be mad, but he's going to lose his shit. He says it unsettles him when he's away from me. I can imagine when he starts to look for me in the office and Christy—poor Christy—tells him that I stepped out. I tried to explain to her that he was going to freak out, but she said she can handle it. I don't think anyone has seen

Daniel freak out before, and I honestly don't know if she's really ready for it.

I take a deep breath as I sit in the waiting room. I've already turned my phone to silent, and I refuse to look at it. I know if I see a missed call from him, I'm going to call him back. I'm weak when it comes to Daniel.

These last couple of months have been off the charts. That night after the bar, Daniel took me home with him. He took care of me, and when I tried to go home the next day, he went with me. He met my father and my mother and darn, I wasn't ready for that. My parents weren't either.

I had no idea what he had planned, but when he told my mom and dad we were getting married and I was moving in with him, I thought my father was going to lose his shit.

I tried to intervene, but Daniel just looked at me with a smile, kissed me on the forehead, and asked to speak to my father privately. Twenty minutes later, my dad was smiling and welcoming Daniel to the family—proving again that he always gets what he wants.

The door from the waiting room leading to the back opens, jarring me back to the present. "Mrs. Chambers?"

I look at the nurse calling my name, and guilt starts to churn in my belly. I stand up and pull my purse over my shoulder, doing my best to smile at the nurse. "That's me."

She returns my smile. "Follow me."

I follow behind her and start to ramble as I do all the pre appointment diagnostics. When I'm finally left in a room, I take a few deep breaths. I sit down in the chair with my hands fidgeting in my lap.

The doctor comes in, and I smile nervously at him. "What's up, Doc?"

He shakes his head and smirks at my joke. "Not much. How you doing today?"

I start to answer him, and then his phone dings in his pocket. He pulls it out and looks at it. He reads it then looks at me over the top of his glasses. "Tell me, is it okay for your husband to come back?"

I imagine that my eyes get as big as saucers. "Uh, I don't..." I start, but I don't get to finish that sentence.

I hear a pounding on the door and then I hear Daniel's voice through the thin wood. "Don't you say it, Sara. So help me if you tell him you don't have a husband I'm going to..."

I roll my eyes, and my face flushes. This is so embarrassing. I jerk open the door. "Geez, are you kidding me right now? Keep it down."

He's mad. Daniel is furious right now. He's looking between the doctor and me, and it's then I find out exactly how smart my doctor is. "Well, I'm going to give you two a few minutes. Just let a nurse know when you're ready for your appointment."

I open my mouth. "I'm ready."

But Daniel shakes his head. "Great, Doc. We'll let you know."

The doctor looks between us and then walks out of the room, shutting the door behind him. Daniel towers over me with a fierce expression on his face. Anyone else would probably be nervous or scared right now, but not me.

I can't help but mess with him. "Did you miss me?"

I swear I can hear the bones in his jaw creak as he answers me. "Don't, Sara. Now's not the time."

I let out a deep breath. "Daniel..."

"You left."

He looks at me as if I just completed some heinous crime or something. I start to laugh, and when his frown deepens, I reach for him. "Daniel... I'm fine. You don't have to follow me everywhere I go."

He looks at me accusingly. "You said you liked it."

I shrug. Honestly, I do, but I know the man needs to work too. "I do... but I wanted to do something. I was wanting to surprise you."

He rubs his hands up and down my arms. "Well, you did that. I was definitely surprised when you snuck out. Poor Christy, I'm going to have to give her a raise."

I cringe because I tried to warn her. I slide my hands up his chest. "How did you know where to find me?"

He shrugs, his face guarded. "I always know where to find you."

I slap him on the chest. "How, Daniel?"

He puts his hand at the nape of my neck. "Don't be mad."

I shrug. It's not like I can stay mad at him anyway. "Okay."

"The app on your phone."

My mouth drops. "You put an app on my phone?"

He pulls his phone from his pocket and shows me the app. "Yes, but you have the same one on yours. All you have to do is open it and you'll know where I'm at all times."

I start to giggle. "It's sort of a waste of an app, really. I always know where you're at... right with me."

"Marry me, Sara."

I open my mouth, and he softly covers it with the palm of his hand. "Hear me out. I love you, you know that. And I know you feel the same. Put me out of my misery and tell me that you'll be my wife."

I start to talk, and he pulls his hand back. "Daniel, the only reason I've held back is because I wanted you to be sure. I didn't want you to change your mind about us ... I wouldn't survive it."

He shakes his head. "Sara, how can you think that? You're it for me. Since the moment I laid eyes on you, you've been the one my heart beats for. Marry me?"

I search his face and see the sincerity there. I've been a fool to put him off. "Yes. I'll marry you."

He pulls me in for a tight hug. His kiss seals over my mouth, and he shows me exactly how much I mean to him. When he pulls away, he's holding up a small box. He opens it and doesn't even hold it out for me to see, he just pulls it out of the box and slides it on my finger. "There."

I look at the ring and up at him. It's the same one he's tried to give me every time he's asked me to marry him. I'm not even surprised that he has it in his pocket. "I love it."

He smiles. "Okay, so now let's talk about this surprise."

I gulp. "It's not much of a surprise now. I mean, what do you get the man that can buy everything he wants? But I mean"—I point to the bed in the middle of the room and then the door—"I don't know anything yet."

He leans his forehead against mine. "You're pregnant, baby."

I gasp. "How do you know that? I mean, I haven't even taken the test or seen the doctor."

He smiles, gesturing to my chest. "Your breasts are bigger and when I touch you"—he slides his hand to the side of my breast and brushes them easily as I jerk—"you're sensitive."

I've hoped, but I wasn't sure. "If I am, you're going to have to marry me sooner rather than later. My dad will not be happy..."

"Done. We'll do it today.... after we leave here."

"Daniel..."

He hugs me against him. "We can have the bigger wedding later, any time you want, but I need you to be my wife now... no more waiting."

I barely get the words out to agree and Daniel's hollering for the doctor down the hallway. When he comes back, the doctor's glasses are on his face sideways and he's straightening them. "Okay, so I guess we're ready then," he says as Daniel lets go of his lab coat.

Thirty minutes later, we're leaving with a little black and white printout of our baby and a prescription for vitamins.

We're standing outside, hovering over the little picture when Daniel breaks the silence. "Are you happy?"

I look at the little miracle on the paper and then up at him. "I can honestly say I've never been happier."

He kisses my lips, holding me close. "I'm going to be even happier when you are my wife."

I stand on my tiptoes and put my arms around his neck. "How come I feel like you're going to stalk me even more now?"

He looks at me innocently. "You can count on it."

"Okay."

His eyebrows raise in surprise. "Okay? You don't mind?"

"I don't mind. I sort of like it."

He leans down and nuzzles into my neck. His hand cups my ass and squeezes as his hot breath brushes my ear. "Good girl."

# Never Been Kissed

Hope Ford

# Chapter 1

---

## *Jared*

I don't second guess myself, I hit send.

I'm sure that Krissy is wondering *"What the hell, why is the nerd from high school contacting me?"* But I figure after all this time, and so many missed opportunities, it is now or never.

My brother Jason is getting married in two days. The photographer cancelled and Jason and his bride-to-be are both freaking out. Without even thinking about it, I told them I knew someone perfect and would take care of it for them. As soon as they said "photographer," Krissy, the woman I've loved since high school, popped into my head. Not that she's ever far from my thoughts, though.

Even back then I knew I was in love with her. And I'm not talking about a small crush that you have and then wake up one day realizing it wasn't for real. No. I'm talking about bona fide, heart-racing love that about takes your breath away.

In high school, she was smart, popular, the homecoming queen and head cheerleader. All of those things are great, but the real her, well, she's amazing. She never had an unkind word for anyone, she didn't care if you were popular or not, she was willing to be your friend. She almost always rooted for the underdog. And when she talked to you, you felt like you were the only person that mattered.

And four years ago, I finally worked up enough nerve to ask her out. I stare at my computer screen, lost in thought about my senior year of high school.

It was one of those rare times that she wasn't surrounded by people. She was walking down the hallway and for the first time her head was hung down low. She was usually smiling at everyone and everything. I stood up straighter, shoved my books into my locker and then shut it easy before striding to the middle of the hallway so I could talk to her.

She kept walking and instead of moving out of the way, I gripped her shoulders. A sob left her lips and I didn't know what to say to her. Talking to people is not really my thing. I went through four years of this school and probably only talked to ten people. I was the class nerd. I wore glasses and I was the smartest person in the school. When she still didn't look up at me, I asked her quietly, "Krissy, are you okay?"

She shrugged her shoulders and because I didn't know what to do, I wrapped my arms around her and hugged her tightly. It was the closest I had ever been to a girl and I could feel my body reacting in unusual ways. I counted to ten in my head, trying to calm myself, but having her in my arms was everything.

She was rigid at first, but then she softened and her arms went around my waist.

I leaned back so I was looking into her face. I brushed the hair away and asked, "What happened? What's wrong?"

"Nothing." She cleared her throat and pulled out of my arms. I wanted to stop her and hold her to me, but I didn't. Her voice was soft and I had to lean in just to hear her. "I'm fine. Sorry for running into you." The corner of her lips lifted into a small smile and then she walked away, with her perfume still lingering around me.

I watched her go. That was the last time that we ever talked. I saw her plenty of times after that, and she would give me a small smile, but she always walked away.

We graduated. She moved away and went to work at a photography studio. I never went to college, it wasn't my thing. I have always been really good with computers and have made money doing online security for major companies. More than enough money to live off of until I'm old and gray.

A ping comes out of the speakers of my laptop. She's replied.

*Jared? My goodness, I can't believe it's you.*

I don't wait. I don't want to lose my nerve. *The photographer for my brother's wedding cancelled. Are you available to shoot it this weekend?*

*As in two days from now?*

*Yes,* I message her back.

*Where's the wedding?*

*Knoxville.*

*I'm in Nashville. I would love to, but I'm trying to open my new studio and funds are tight right now. I'm sorry. I would have loved to have seen you.*

I start to type 'I know' but quickly delete it. Her profile doesn't have her location on it and I'm sure if I tell her I know she's in Nashville then she's going to know something's up. The truth is, I've kept tabs on her the last four years. Well, electronic tabs. I know everything she posts, the storefront she's looking at, hell, I follow her Pinterest board and know exactly what she wants her studio to look like, her future house to look like. I know way more than I probably should. But I can't apologize for it.

I'm trying not to sound desperate, but I have to get her here. I need to come up with something and quick. I'm going to pay her and I about type $50k but I figure that would probably scare her off. That's a little crazy even for me. Even though I've seen her work and she is one of the best.

*I would pay you. I figure if you travel here for the rehearsal dinner, the wedding and if you could stay a* *few days afterwards I would love to have you take some pictures of property I'm trying to sell. $25,000? And of course I'll pay for travel, food and lodging.*

Her profile moves down the message so I know she has seen it. But after a few seconds, she doesn't reply.

$30,000? I type and hit send. I don't even think about it, I'll pay whatever I have to to get her here.

The little bubble pops up to let me know she's typing. *No! That's crazy. If you pay for lodging, food and travel I will do it for free. I don't feel right charging you.*

### Krissy

You want to talk about a surprise. I can't believe it's been four years since I've seen or heard from Jared and when I do he's offering to pay me $30,000 to come and take pictures. How does he even know I'm a photographer now?

Jared was always quiet in school. He usually had his nose in a book or a computer. He was nice to me though. I think back to my senior year. I had just found out my parents were getting a divorce and fell apart in the hallway. He held me, and I swear I can still remember how it felt to be in his arms. After that, I was embarrassed. I had always liked him, but I knew he didn't think of me like that so I avoided him.

*$30K Krissy. That's the deal. Can you fly out Friday morning?*

I should probably tell him yes to the money. I could definitely use it. It would be a big help, but I was honest when I told him that I didn't feel right letting him pay me. I know we weren't close in high school. But to this day, I've always thought of him as a friend.

*Yes. We'll talk about payment when I get there.*

*I'll send you the travel itinerary, tickets and traveling money in the morning.*

I stare at my computer and the bubbles pop up letting me know he's typing something. *I can't wait to see you again, Krissy.*

I sit back in my chair and insecurity comes over me. I shouldn't let it and normally I wouldn't but I want him to like me. I look down at the extra padding on my stomach and thighs. He's probably expecting the cheerleader from high school and that's not who I am. Not anymore.

I close my laptop and lie down, dreaming of him.

# Chapter 2

## *Jared*

I arrived at the airport an hour early. I wanted to make sure I had time to park and wait for her. I'm standing next to the security line, watching passengers arrive. Her plane just landed and she should be walking by any time now. I scan the crowd looking for her. There are people squealing, hugging each other and excited around me, but I don't take my eyes off the revolving door.

When I see someone with long blond hair behind a taller man, my body instantly tightens. I know it's her. I don't take my eyes off her. The man walking beside her is talking to her and she laughs. My fists clench at my sides, but it doesn't sway me.

She looks up when she gets twenty feet away and even from here I can see the surprise on her face. She stumbles and the man next to her holds her up. I barely contain my growl before I stride over to them.

I stand before her awkwardly. We just stand here, people walking all around us. The man that was next to her walks on after telling her bye. She doesn't even notice.

"Jared?" Shock fills her voice. "Is that you? I mean of course it's you, but you look so different. My God." She says those words and then looks down my body. When her eyes climb back up me and land on mine again, she smacks her hands across her mouth.

I smile at her and take my turn to look down her body. She too is different from high school. But I already know that since I follow her on all her social media. She has on tennis shoes, leggings and a wide neck red shirt. I try not to stare at her breasts before moving back up to her eyes. "Krissy, you're even more beautiful."

I open my arms to hug her and she hesitates briefly before entering my embrace. I hold on to her then. The feel of her sweet curves against me has my cock hardening in my pants.

I pull back from her, not wanting to embarrass her.

Her face is flushed and she tugs at the bottom of her shirt. "Yeah, I'm a little different from high school, too. Not the cheerleader anymore."

I turn my head sideways, trying to understand what she's saying. I may look the jock part now, but I'm still not completely sure about all the social niceties. When she won't look into my eyes, I guess that she's embarrassed... maybe because she's gained some weight since high school.

But do you tell a woman you like her curves? The longer I stand here not saying anything, the more her face turns a darker shade of red.

Finally, I ball up and just say what I'm thinking. "You were beautiful in high school, Krissy, but nothing could have prepared me to see you now. You're breathtakingly beautiful... plus, I love curves... especially yours."

Her eyes flick to mine and I see how much she appreciates what I said. I finally take a breath, one I didn't know I was holding.

"Should we go get your luggage?" I ask her and place my hand at the small of her back to lead her to the baggage claim.

"So what do you do, Jared?" she asks me.

"I do online security," I tell her.

"Online, huh? I guess that explains how I had two thousand dollars in my account this morning. Do you always hack into people's bank accounts?"

Laughing at her question, I try not to tense up. If only she knew what all I've hacked into. "I needed to get you the travel money. I figured that was the easiest way."

"Yeah, I'm not even going to ask how you got my account number. I should be freaked out," she admits, smiling up at me. I didn't realize how short she was. Looking down at her small stature, I can't stop the feelings of protectiveness coming through me.

We stop walking when we get to the luggage conveyor belt. "I would never do anything to hurt you, Krissy."

He shrugs. "I would worry about you being at a hotel by yourself. At least at my house you would be close by and I could make sure you're okay."

I laugh. "I'm a big girl."

He nods his head. "You're right. I'm sorry. I didn't mean to make it awkward."

I think about it for a minute, and decide why not? "Okay... I'd like to stay with you."

He turns to me with the biggest grin on his face. "Really?"

"Yeah, sure, it will give us more time to catch up. Plus, it's not like I just met you or anything. I trust you."

He smiles all the way to his house. Every time I look at him, his grin widens.

We talk small talk, and I ask him about the bride. I remember his older brothers, but I didn't know them well.

"Well, Jason is a baseball player now. He met his fiancée, Chelsey, at one of the ballgames and they fell in love. It's been quick, but she's going to fit into the family just fine. "

"Were they okay with you asking me to take the pictures?" I've thought about this a lot. I don't know any bride that would just turn the task of finding a photographer over to their soon-to-be brother in law.

"Sure, she actually begged me once I showed her your portfolio."

"My portfolio? You been stalking me, Mr. Blake?"

He winces, but then covers it up with a smile. "Maybe."

# Chapter 3

*Jared*

Once we arrive at my house, I take her on a tour. I explain to her this is one of the properties that I'll be selling and I'll want her to take pictures while she's here.

I show her the inground pool, the guest house, and when we get back inside she's twirling around looking at everything. "Jared, this house is stunning. Why are you selling it?"

"If everything goes as planned, I will be moving soon, so I need to go ahead and get the house on the market."

I can see the question in her eyes, but she doesn't ask it. Which is probably good. How do I explain to her that I'm planning on moving to Nashville to be closer to her? She'd probably run screaming from the house.

I show her to her room. I could have given her a room on the opposite side of the house but instead I give her the one across from mine. The temptation will kill me, I'm sure, but I want her close.

I leave her to freshen up for the rehearsal dinner and I go to take a cold shower. The first of many, I'm sure.

An hour later, I'm standing at the front door, trying to tie my tie.

"I wasn't sure. Do I look okay?" she asks from the top of the stairs. I drop my hands to my sides and turn to face her. She's walking down the stairs in black dress pants, black heels, and a royal blue sparkly blouse. Her hair is in long curly waves down her back. I wish I could say screw it and keep her here to myself.

"You're beautiful," I tell her honestly. Her blue eyes sparkle back at me.

"I normally would wear a skirt, but if I'm taking pictures, I didn't want to be showing the world my undies while doing so."

I suck in a breath at the mere mention of her panties. Yeah, fuck that, no one needs to be seeing that—no one but me.

I mutter, "Yeah, I'd hate to have to gouge some man's eyes out."

"What was that?"

I turn back to the mirror. "Oh nothing, I'm having trouble with my tie."

She's standing at my shoulder, looking at me in the mirror. "Let me help you."

I turn to face her, and she lifts the tie and ties it perfectly. When she's done, she smooths it down my flat stomach, and I barely hold my groan in. With her hands on me, standing this close to me, I have no control over myself..

She steps backward, putting some distance between us, and I release the breath I didn't know I was holding.

"Thank you." I hold my arm out to her. "Ready?"

She picks up her bags of photo equipment and nods her head. I grab the bags from her and she loops her arm through mine.

The drive to the church for the rehearsal practice only takes a few minutes. I can tell she's nervous, so I try to get her talking about the studio she wants to open. She opens up then and I can hear the excitement in her voice. "I've wanted this for so long. I may have to put it off for a while, but it's a dream I plan on making happen. I even have the perfect spot picked out in downtown Nashville. It is right off the main street, so it's close but not too close. I'm hoping that it stays empty for a little longer. I think I just need a few more weeks before I would be ready... fingers crossed."

"I'm sure you'll be a success, Krissy," I tell her honestly. I want to tell her not to worry about the building, but I can't. Not without giving my secret away. And I'm not ready to do that yet.

The church is full of family when we get there and immediately the wedding planner starts telling everyone what to do and where they need to be. I leave Krissy at a seat to take my position up at the altar next to my brother. I wanted to introduce her to everyone, but they are already in the thick of things. Besides a quick head nod and slap on the back with my brother, we are down to business.

The rehearsal goes quickly and I know I should be paying closer attention, but my eyes are on Krissy. She's moving around, not getting in the way, but getting shots of everyone. She's completely in her element and the joy on her face makes her even more beautiful.

After a quick run through, we drive over to the hotel where the dinner is being held. When we pull up, I hand my keys to the valet and rush around the truck, waving off the man about to open the door for her. I help her down and grab her bags out of the back. Once we get inside, it's a whirlwind. Everyone is so excited to meet Krissy and she and Chelsey get caught up talking about the pictures she wants.

Everyone sits down to eat, but Krissy walks around the room capturing photos of the group. I ignore the people around me. Which isn't uncommon for me. I'm always the quiet one that doesn't have a lot to say, so no one is surprised by it. Because I can't stand it anymore, I fix her a plate and take it to her. "Here. You haven't eaten since you got off the plane."

She smiles at me and eyes the plate. "I'm working, Jared. I can't eat."

I grab her by the hand and I can see the surprise in her face. "C'mon, ten minutes. You have to eat something. I should have fed you earlier. I'm sorry, I don't know what I was thinking."

She lets me lead her to a corner of the room and we sit next to each other at a small table. I set the plate down in front of her. She sets down her camera and looks back at me. "Oh, I'm sorry, I guess you need your hand back." I release her hand, and want to kick myself for being so awkward.

She looks at me and my face flushes. "I don't know. I kinda like holding your hand, Jared."

When I don't respond, the smile drops off her face and she concentrates on her plate, taking a bite of the steak medallion.

I scoot my chair closer to her and hold my hand out to her. When she sees it, she gently places her hand in mine and lays our joined hands down on her thigh. She smiles as she takes another bite of food.

*Krissy*

Jared's whole family is amazing and just by meeting Jason and Chelsey, I know that this is going to be one of the most beautiful weddings I've ever done.

We get back to Jared's house late and before I go upstairs to bed, I have to bring it up. "Jared, I think we need to talk about something."

His eyes get big and worried, but I assure him it's okay. "I just need to talk to you about the picture fee. Look, thirty thousand dollars is ridiculous. I'm not taking that amount of money from you for this. And Chelsey told me you offered to foot the bill for the photographer. Please, the money you have already put into my account will cover expenses. I can show you my packages I offer and you can order from that for the rest."

He's shaking his head. "Let's not talk about this now, okay? I know you've had a long day and we have a big day tomorrow. We'll talk about this later."

I laugh at him. "Well, I've already seen how you can make money magically appear into someone's account. That's why I thought we should figure it out now."

He's put his hand at the small of my back and leads me up the stairs. He opens the bedroom door and sets down my bags on the dresser before turning around to face me. "Don't be mad, okay?"

"What did you do?" I ask him incredulously.

"I already put the money in your account. But I promise, I'm going to have you so busy the next few days, you are probably going to need to ask for more."

I put my hands on my hip and cock it out. "That's ridiculous. I don't feel right taking that money from you... especially now."

"What do you mean, especially now?"

I get all flustered. I can't tell him because I have feelings for him, or that I always have. "I just can't. It's not right."

He's quiet for a long time and when I look up into his face, I see the vulnerability there. This massive, strong handsome man is vulnerable. "Are you mad at me?" he asks me.

"No," I whisper. "But I'm going to give you some of that money back."

His shoulders drop and he walks to the door. He takes one last look at me before walking out. "I'll see you in the morning, Krissy. Sleep well."

As soon as the door closes, I stride over to it. I reach for the handle to pull it open, but at the last minute, I stop myself. What am I going to say to him? *Wait... don't leave. Stay... take my virginity?*

Yep, that's right. I'm a twenty-two-year-old virgin. Not that I haven't had the opportunity. I've just never found someone that I was really attracted to, no one that makes my heart race like Jared does.

Walking to the bed, I toss myself onto it, grab the pillow and groan into it.

# Chapter 4

## *Jared*

We're at the church again the next morning and I can't take my eyes off her. She's taken all the shots of the groom and groomsmen and the bride and bridesmaids. Now we're just waiting on the bride to show up. When she doesn't, it seems that all hell breaks loose.

Jason is a mess. Luckily, our other brother, Jack, Jason's twin, showed up this morning and he is exactly what Jason needs. They've always had a connection. I send them on their way and I take care of letting the guests know that there won't be a wedding today.

Around mid afternoon, once I have the parents calmed down and the guests have left, I take Krissy back to my house, but I don't know how to process all of this. Anyone that knows Chelsey knows how much she loves Jason. None of it makes sense.

"Jared." Krissy clears her throat. "Uh, I understand if you need to be alone. I can get an earlier flight."

"No." I realize she probably thinks I'm upset with her and soften my voice. "I'd like for you to stay with me. If that's okay?"

She stares back at me for a second and then nods.

We walk into the house and I sit down on the couch, my elbows on my knees and my head in my hands. For a person that doesn't do emotions well, I'm feeling a little overwhelmed.

I feel the heat of Krissy's body as she sits down on the coffee table in front of me, her legs fitted between mine.

Her hand goes to the back of my neck, and I feel her knead the muscles there. A deep groan escapes my lips, but she doesn't stop. If anything, she deepens the pressure.

I lift my head to look at her, wanting to tell her so much, but not knowing how. "Can I hold you,

Krissy?"

I don't even recognize my voice when I ask her that. Her eyes widen, but she simply nods her head. I lean back on the couch and pull her hands to tug her into my lap. She sits sideways on me and the feel of her against me fills me with a satisfaction that I haven't felt before. It just feels right.

I wrap my arms around her and bury my nose against her neck. She's holding herself tightly, and I'm worried that I've pushed her too far, or maybe made her uncomfortable.

"I'm sorry, honey. Is this weird for you? I just needed to hold you, but if you're uncomfortable..."

She interrupts me, lifting her eyes to look at mine. "No. No, I'm fine. I just don't want to hurt you."

"Hurt me? Honey, you couldn't hurt me," I tell her honestly.

She looks at me and I can tell that she's trying to see if I'm being sincere. When I don't look away, she must read it in my eyes or maybe she feels the way my grip on her tightens, because finally she seems to relax, and she wraps herself around my body.

It isn't long before she's asleep in my arms, and I sit there staring at her with hope rising in my chest.

*Krissy*

We must have been asleep for a few hours, because the sun is already starting to set. My stomach growls and I hold in a giggle because I'm now sprawled on top of Jared on the couch.

My head is resting on his chest, and his arms are wrapped around me. I lift my head and rest my chin on his pec, looking up at him. He's still asleep, but even now, I can tell he's frustrated because his forehead is drawn together. I reach up, slowly, and put my lips to his chin, lightly kissing him. I wish I could take away his worry.

He lifts his knee up, and my body slides closer to his. His hands stroke down my back and cup my cheeks. Still, I don't take my eyes off him. I think he's still asleep. I feel his hips lift underneath me and I can feel his hard cock press into my belly.

I lay perfectly still, not wanting to wake him, but also feeling like I should. I lay my head back down on his chest and as if I'm wanting to test him, I shove my hips into him and a deep groan leaves his lips. I smile against his chest.

I feel his body tauten underneath me and I try to lay completely still against him.

"Krissy," he whispers against the top of my head.

I move my body slowly against his, acting like I'm just waking up. His hands instantly tightens on my ass and he holds me forcefully, stopping me from making any movements.

"Honey, I don't know if I can take much more of this."

"Of what?" I ask him innocently.

"Of your curvy body rubbing against me."

I climb off of him, ignoring his groans as I move across him. I stand next to the couch and his hooded eyes stare up at me. He grabs on to my hand, pulls himself up and stands up next to me. "I like having you in my arms, Krissy."

Those words are everything to me, and I almost repeat the same thing back to him. But of course, my stomach has the worst timing and growls again.

He chuckles. "C'mon, we better eat."

After dinner, where he had me put together a salad and he grilled chicken, we set down on the couch to watch a movie.

"You okay?" I ask him for the twentieth time.

He sets down his phone. "Yeah, Jason thinks that she went on the honeymoon. He's on a flight there now."

"I hope everything is okay."

He nods his head. "Yeah, me too."

"So, tomorrow, do you want me to take pictures of your house?"

He's sitting on the couch a few feet away. "That would be great."

We watch television for a while until we both go to bed. The chemistry between us is explosive and I don't think either one of us knows what to do with it.

The next day, we spend the whole day together. He feeds me breakfast, then we take pictures of the land and the house, then we go sightseeing and out to dinner. There are times I almost hold his hand, but stopped myself.

# Chapter 5

## *Jared*

Later that night, as we're about to go to our separate bedrooms, I stop her.

"Will I go to Miami with you?" she asks me. I've completely caught her off guard.

I explain to her briefly, "Yeah, so come to find out, Jack wasn't supposed to have been able to make the wedding. Well, when Chelsey saw Jack kissing a woman outside the church, she thought it was Jason. Anyway, Jack texted and said the family needs to be there by tomorrow afternoon for the wedding."

"And you want me to go with you... to take pictures?" she asks again.

She's standing in the open doorway of the bedroom, leaning against the door jamb, her arms crossed over her body. I take a step toward her. "Well, I would like for you to be my date for the wedding actually."

Her expression instantly transforms and her happiness is shining on her face. "Okay."

"Really?... I mean, great, so we'll leave in the morning."

I turn around to walk across the hall and when I get to my door, she calls my name. "Yeah?" I ask her and when I turn around, I notice that she's standing right next to me.

She gets up on her tiptoes, wraps her hand around the back of my neck and pulls me down to her. Her lips brush across mine and I feel the jolt through my whole body. My hands go to her thick hips, gripping on to her and pulling her into me.

Our kiss deepens and the taste and smell of her surround me, burning me up inside. She pulls back from me and her hand goes to her mouth. She's smiling widely at me.

"That was my first kiss... well, I don't count little Bobby Ray back in kindergarten. I punched him afterwards."

I'm trying to catch my breath, and I barely register what she's saying. But then it hits me, I'm her first kiss... and she's mine.

"Mine too," I admit to her and I feel heat flush my face.

"What? No way!" She laughs and swats me across the chest, turning away from me. I grab her hand so I don't let her go far.

"No, I promise, you were my first. I wouldn't lie to you." I try not to wince at my declaration. Technically, I haven't lied to her. Not about the kissing, but about other stuff—well, I've withheld information, maybe.

"Well, that's crazy. Look at you."

I pull her closer, fitting her curves against me, leaning my forehead against hers. "I can say the same thing to you, honey."

"I want to do it again, Jared," she huskily whispers.

I don't hesitate; I lean in and capture her lips with mine.

When we finally break away, we're both breathing heavily. We're still standing in the hallway and I just hold her to me, feeling her body calm against mine.

"Uh, we better go to bed, I mean, I better go to my bed and you to your bed." She laughs.

I kiss the top of her head, then step back from her. "Yeah, you're right, so I'll see you in the morning."

I watch her walk into her bedroom and she takes one last peak at me before shutting the door behind her.

I walk into my bedroom, and instantly I undo my jeans, pulling them and my underwear down until I'm standing there with my dick in my hand. I'm so hard it's painful. I've never felt such sweet torture in my life. All I have to think about is her beautiful face, her curvy body and I'm already about to come. I stroke myself, imagining her in my arms, her lips wrapped around my cock, and my balls tighten as hot ropes of cum shoot from my dick. I release a guttural moan. "Krissy."

My body's heaving and I'm leaning on the dresser to hold myself up. A part of me didn't want to come. I wanted to save it for her, but I couldn't. Having her this close to me is going to kill me. I take a ragged deep breath and stumble to the bathroom to clean myself up.

*Krissy*

I come back out of my room and walk across the hall. I lift my hand to knock when I hear groaning on the other side. I hold my ear to the door, and I know exactly what I hear. Jared's breathing is choppy and it isn't long before I hear a loud groan from his room and him saying my name.

My insides turn to mush. If I had any doubt, I know for sure now, he wants me. And I want him. I pull back from the door and walk back to my room. I lay down in the bed and all my thoughts go to him. He's come out of his shell since high school. Well, some anyway. He doesn't have any trouble talking to me, but he doesn't seem to talk to anyone else a whole lot.

If I go back to Nashville a virgin, not experiencing the one thing I know I want, have wanted for so long, I know I'll regret it. I can't let that happen.

I lay back in the bed thinking of the way Jared kissed me. I never would have guessed it was his first kiss. Of course, what do I know?

But we seemed to have a connection. My hand dips into my panties. I'm soaked, from his kiss and from hearing him grunt my name, I'm sure. My fingers slide across my throbbing clit and my hips flex uncontrollably. I reach further down, coating my finger in my fresh juices and then I put more pressure on my swollen clit, rubbing circles around it. A moan escapes me, and I bite my lower lip to contain myself. Aww, yes. I keep stroking until my hips are gyrating and I've worked myself into a frenzy. "Yes. Aww, Jared," I exclaim as I climax and my body clenches as my pussy pulsates around my hand.

I curl to my side with my hand still between my legs. I cover my face, trying to control my erratic heartbeat and tremors shaking through my body. I can count the number of times I've done that on probably two hands, but I've never came so fast and so hard before.

It's all Jared. I know it is. I fall asleep and have the most erotic dreams of my life.

# Chapter 6

## *Jared*

Ever since she woke up this morning, she's been quiet and subdued. I was planning on continuing where we left off last night with a kiss this morning, but when I walked into the kitchen and she was pouring a cup of coffee, she would barely look at me.

We're strolling through the airport and I'm pulling our luggage behind me. "Where are we going?" she asks as I stride in the opposite direction of the terminals.

"We're taking a private jet," I tell her.

She gasps, "You have a private jet?"

"Well, it's not mine, but I'm able to use it any time I want. It's one of the perks of working with one of my clients," I tell her.

Honestly, I should have offered to take the whole family with me. But I stopped myself. I want as much time alone with Krissy as I can get. I'm not good with people anyway, but I'm really not good with sharing her.

We walk down the tarmac and a man meets us and takes the luggage, and a woman escorts us on to the plane. I have my hand at the small of Krissy's back as if I'm helping her, but really I just need to touch her.

When we get inside, she's amazed by it all. She walks up and down the aisle, all the way to the back of the plane where there is a small bedroom and bathroom, and comes back out with her mouth hanging open. "Oh my God, Jared, there's a bedroom back here. And a bathroom that is probably as big as my bedroom and living room combined."

I laugh at her words, but secretly it bothers me. Krissy deserves the best and I want her to have that.

The announcement comes on, asking us to prepare for takeoff. We sit down and I help her with her seatbelt.

She's subdued again and I don't try to talk to her until we are up in the air.

"Did I upset you last night, Krissy?"

Her hands are in her lap, wrapped around each other.

"No. You didn't upset me at all." She smiles at me and I turn in the seat next to her.

"Are you sure? I didn't want to pressure you or anything," I ask again. I don't ever want to make her uncomfortable.

"I wasn't. I'm not. I mean... well, I liked it when you kissed me. Is that what you're asking about?" she stutters.

I try to hide the shock on my face. I nod my head at her.

There's a ding and the little light goes off, letting us know that we can remove our seatbelts.

She releases hers and stands up in front of me, holding her hand out to me. "Jared, will you come with me?"

I look between her flushed face and her outstretched hand. I undo my seatbelt and put my hand in hers. She leads me to the back of the plane, into the bedroom, and then shuts the door behind us.

"Krissy?" I ask her hesitantly. I don't want her to think she has to do this.

"Wait, Jared." She holds her hand up to stop me. "Let me get this out. I have to. I've liked you since high school. And I've thought about you a lot these last four years since then. I don't want to go back to my life like it was. I want to experience this with you."

I kiss her, because I have to. I devour her mouth with mine. When I feel like I can't get close enough to her, even with our mouths and bodies meshed together, I pick her up by her hips and her legs lock around me. I carry her to the bed and lay her back gently. Standing over her, I can't believe how beautiful she is. I am still caught up by her perfection.

I undo the button on her jeans and strip them down her legs. She takes off her blue sweater and throws it across the room. She's lying before me in a pair of skimpy black panties and a lacy black bra.

I slide my fingers into the side of her panties and draw them slowly down her legs. Her thighs close back together after I get a brief glimpse of her pussy. Her bra luckily snaps in the front and I start to undo it, clumsily, until she takes pity on me and removes it on her own. When she's completely bare beneath me, I put my hands on her knees and slide her legs apart.

Her damp curls at her apex part, and her swollen, wet slit is tantalizing me. I inhale deeply, almost like I can imagine what she smells like just by looking at her.

I slide up on the bed between her thighs and when she sees where I'm going she tries to stop me. "You don't have to do that."

"Honey, my God, I want to. I want to taste you more than I want to breathe right now," I grunt, forcing her legs farther apart and settling between them. I nibble down her inner thigh, trying to recall all the research I've done on this. I always dreamed about this, but never really thought it would happen. But just in case, I wanted to make sure I knew what I was doing. When I reach her bare center, I tentatively swipe my tongue across her drenched, swollen slit. Her taste hits my tongue and it's like instinct takes over. I dive into her, caressing every part of her with my hands, my mouth, my tongue. I can't get enough of her. I slide my hands under her ass and raise her up until I'm eating her pussy, suckling all her fresh juices that are coating my tongue. I slide my tongue to her swollen clit and stroke her there.

Her hand goes to the back of my head, gripping my hair roughly and then holding me to her while she lifts her hips up and down. She's moaning, saying my name over and over, begging me not to stop. As if I could.

When her body tightens underneath me and her legs lock around my neck, I still don't stop until she's screaming her release, and screaming MY name. If I wasn't trying to concentrate on not coming in my jeans, I would be bowing my chest out like a proud peacock. I just made her come.

I lean up a little and lay my head down on her belly. We're both breathing hard, trying to catch our breath.

She wiggles out from underneath me and rolls me on my back. Her breasts move and shake with every movement, making my mouth water. I lean up and nip her pointy peak between my lips, but she pulls back from me. "Oh no, mister. Your turn."

She reaches for my zipper and starts to unzip me. But I stop her with my hand. "No, I don't want our first time to be on an airplane. I want to be able to take more than an hour with you, honey."

She rears back and looks at me and a smile forms on her face. "Okay. I agree, but that doesn't mean that I can't please you."

She starts pulling my jeans down, and I start stuttering, "No, really, this can wait. You don't have to do this."

But she doesn't stop, not until my shoes, pants and underwear are thrown on the floor and she's standing between my legs with her hands covering her mouth.

"Oh, my God, Jared."

I lift up on my elbows, looking between my hard cock that is covered in precum and her surprised face.

"What is it? What's wrong?" I ask her.

"Is that normal? I've never seen one before," she asks.

I smirk. "You mean normal size?"

She merely nods her head, not taking her eyes off it.

"Maybe a little bigger than normal," I admit to her. "But when the time comes, it will fit."

She looks at me unsure, but then drops slowly to her knees, staring at it.

*Krissy*

I gather in close to him, feeling his warmth surround me. His penis is thick and long. It's veiny and almost purple looking, with cum leaking from its tip.

I lean in close to him, my hands on his thighs, and touch my tongue to his tip. He gasps and shocked, I look up into his wide eyes. "Honey, I'm not going to last long. I'm sorry."

His face is pinched in either embarrassment or trying to control himself. Maybe a little bit of both.

"That's probably good, because I don't know what I'm doing," I admit to him.

He takes a deep breath. "You can't do anything wrong. Not with me. And if you don't want to, you don't have to." He pulls a stray hair away from my face.

The look he's giving me makes me want to please him. "I want to," I whisper to him before touching him again.

I swirl my tongue across his tip, tasting his hot primal seed. I stroke him from root to tip and just by paying attention to his sounds, I can tell what he likes.

So when he moans, I do the same thing again, harder and with more pressure. When I have him as far down my throat as I can get him, I back off to the tip and then swallow him again. With each up and down, I tighten my grip on him, sucking him deeper and deeper until I can feel him hitting the back of my throat. His hands grip my forearms, and with his cock still in my mouth, I look up at him. One clash of our glance has his orgasm speeding out of control and he's pumping his hips against my face. I don't take my eyes off him, I can't. He's handsome, but when he's losing control, when I'm the one that's causing him to lose control and his face is pinched in desire all because of me, well, an electric charge fills my body and I don't stop pleasuring him until he's come deep into my throat and I'm swallowing his seed down.

I roll off of him and lie on my back next to him.

"Honey, after the wedding, I'm taking you to the room and I'm making good on my promise."

I take a deep breath, trying to stop my ragged breathing. "What promise is that?"

"The promise I made myself that if I ever had you, I would make it so good for you that you would want me in your life forever."

I blink back the tears after hearing what he just said, I know these feelings I have for him are something special. This doesn't happen just every day or with just anyone. "I'm pretty sure I already want that, Jared."

## Chapter 7

### *Jared*

Once we're off the plane, everything happens in fast motion. We go to the wedding and while everyone is watching the bride and groom, I'm watching Krissy. She moves around us all taking everyone's pictures. She's even more beautiful today. Her confidence is off the charts and after the ceremony when she comes up next to me and slides her hand in mine, well, I know then, that I have to hold her. The brief time we had on the plane wasn't enough.

We all go out to dinner together, even though I did everything I could to get out of it. Finally, my brothers' guilting me had me showing up. Krissy shakes her head at me, knowing exactly why I want to skip out on this meal. She pats me on the chest and then whispers to me, "It's okay, stud. We have the rest of our lives. Enjoy your family."

I hold her hand through the whole meal, and when I finally see an opening, I pull her from the dinner and take her back to the room.

As soon as we cross the threshold, I wrap my arms around her and ravage her mouth with a kiss. She pulls away from me briefly, then leans in to kiss me again before quickly pulling back. "I need to freshen up."

I nod my head and reluctantly let her go.

I pace around the room and finally sit down on the bed, removing my shoes, coat and tie. I would take off the rest, but I don't want to look impatient when she comes out of the bathroom.

When I hear the door open, I look at her coming out in a robe. She looks like a woman on a mission, but I can see the hesitancy in her eyes. When she stops right before me, she lets the robe fall from her shoulders and she's standing before me in white underwear and a white bra. Her curvy body is perfection and as I take her in, I don't know where to start.

"Are you sure about this, Krissy?" I ask her, while simultaneously praying that she doesn't change her mind.

She nods her head, unbuttoning my shirt and pulling it off my shoulders. She roams her hands all across my chest, and each caress causes me to flex underneath her soft hands.

"You're beautiful, honey. The most beautiful woman I've ever seen," I tell her honestly, before reaching behind her and undoing her bra, then peeling it from her body. I palm her large breasts and bend down, sucking one nipple into my mouth, while massaging the other one with my hand. Her arms go to my shoulders and she holds on to me tightly. When her head falls back, and I eye her exposed neck, I move up her body, licking her cleavage, her neck and her earlobe.

My hands dip into the front of her panties, and with one swipe, she coats my hand with her flowing juices.

"Fuck, yeah," I moan against her.

I yank her panties down her legs, and when she steps out of them, I lay her back on the bed.

I remove my shirt, jeans and underwear, stroking my cock with my hand as I watch her hooded eyes glance across my body.

"I can't wait any longer to make you mine, Krissy."

"I don't want you to." She holds her arms out to me and I go to her. I lean down and press my lips to hers. Pulling her to the edge of the bed, I bend her knees and hook them over my shoulders. I start kissing her inner thigh and her soft mound.

"No," she mutters.

I raise up and look at her with dread in my eyes. "No?"

"I'm ready. Feel how wet I am, Jared. This is all I've thought about all day. I'm tired of waiting. I want you inside me. Now," she begs of me.

I nod my head, looking at her glistening exposed pussy. I line my cock up at her center and stroke through her lips, coating my cock with her juices. Her warmth is everything and I can already feel myself starting to lose control.

I enter her slowly, taking deep breaths. Her heat surrounds me and she clenches on to me tightly. I can barely move, her pussy is strangling me so tightly.

"Honey, I don't want to hurt you." I slowly start to withdraw, but her legs bend around me and I feel her heels pressing on my ass, holding me there.

"No. You won't hurt me. I want this. I want you, Jared. Please."

She arches her back and pushes herself up until I'm sliding farther into her. It's too much, fuck, it's too much. I never imagined it would feel like this.

When I reach her threshold, I stop and look down at her passion-filled face. Her eyes are begging me for more. I lean down and kiss her before I plow into her, sinking my rod into her tight pussy. Her mouth opens under mine in a scream, but I don't pull back. I whisper against her lips, "Are you okay? Do you want me to stop?"

"No, God, no, please don't stop."

When she feels like she's adjusted to me, I start moving inside her. She moans my name with each thrust and I start counting back from ten because I can't hold back much longer.

I reach between us and rub her clit with my thumb while I take her pussy with long strokes. She's writhing underneath me and when she tenses up, putting my cock into a vise grip, I come when she does, and we both climax together.

I don't want to hurt her, so I pull out of her slowly. Her little pussy tingles around me and I can feel the aftershocks of her orgasm, sliding across my dick.

The proof of her virginity is on my dick and her inner thighs and I stand there looking at it, wanting to commit it to memory. Call me a sick bastard if you want, but she just gave me what no man will ever have. She's mine now and the proof is on my dick.

I go to the bathroom before coming back to her and gently cleaning her up. When I slide into bed next to her, she's already almost asleep. I wrap myself around her and fall asleep dreaming of the future.

# Chapter 8

## *Krissy*

I stretch in the bed, feeling muscles pull that I didn't even know I had. I hear the shower running and sit up in the bed. Smiling, I think I might surprise him in the shower. I start walking toward the bathroom, naked, when something on his open laptop catches my eye.

I get closer to the desk and bend over, not touching anything, but wanting to get a closer look. I bend down and look at it and sure enough, there's an icon on his computer that says "Krissy."

Curiosity gets the better of me and I click on the mouse, scrolling over to my name to open it. What I see guts me.

The file is full of everything about me. Letters between my first boss out of high school and Jared. All of my debt I've had over the years, and somehow have gotten paid off or I've won some kind of prize that I don't remember playing for. There's papers on the building I'm looking at for my studio, and negotiations for its lease. There's pictures of me from my social media and even a picture of me winning a photography award two years ago. My mind can't keep up with it all. Everything from my whole last four years are in a little folder on his laptop. I'm trying to read it all and I don't realize that Jared has come out of the bathroom until he says, "Let me explain, Krissy."

I jump up from the chair and realize I'm still naked. I spot the robe on the floor and shrug into it. I can't have this conversation now. Not now.

"I'm going to shower. Then I want to go home," I tell him and stomp off to the bathroom.

When I come out, twenty minutes later, Jared stands up with his hands out in front of me. "Please, let's talk about this."

"There's nothing to talk about. You have stalked me. You have controlled the last four years of my life and

I didn't even know it. How dumb am I? Really, I believed that some prize money paid off my car." I shake my head. "I'm so stupid." I stop and point my finger at him. "Did you pull strings for me to win the photography award?"

He instantly shakes his head. "No, no. I promise. You did that on your own."

I turn my head to the side and eye him speculatively. I shake my head again, unable to wrap my head around it. I start throwing everything into a bag. "I'm leaving, Jared."

He stops me. "That's fine. You want to leave. I understand. But I'm flying you home and making sure you get there safely."

I shrug my shoulders and stomp from the room.

With every stomp through the hotel and the airport, I start to realize that I'm throwing a tantrum. The plane ride home, I'm fuming. I can't believe that he did all of this. I don't even know what to believe anymore.

The plane ride is tense and when he tries to talk to me, I completely ignore him. My heart is shattering in my chest and I'm doing everything I can not to break down right now.

Once we land, I grab my bags from his hand. "I'm home safe. You can leave now."

I turn to walk away and he follows me until we get outside.

"Krissy. Listen, I'm going to make sure you get home. I'm not leaving you like this, then I'll leave you alone if that's what you want." He guts me when he says that, but I hold the sob in and nod my head.

A towncar is waiting for us and I slide into the seat. He helps the man stow the luggage and then slides in next to me. I almost tell him where I live and then realize he already knows it.

I lean my head back and close my eyes, ready for this day to already come to an end.

*Jared*

I know I've freaked her out and I don't know how to fix it. But I know I have to try.

When we stowed the luggage, I asked the driver to take us to the location of the studio she wants. Luckily, she has her eyes closed the whole way and doesn't realize where we're going.

She lifts her head when we park. "Jared, what are we doing here?"

I get out of the car and lean in, holding my hand out for her. "Let me show you something."

She eyes my hand but doesn't move.

"Please, this will be the last thing I ask of you."

She ignores my hand and slides from the car.

I open the door to her studio and stand back, letting her walk in first.

As soon as she walks in, she gasps and her hands go to her mouth. Already tears are streaming down her face.

A man walks into the room from the back. "Mr. Blake, I'm so sorry. I thought I had a few more days to get everything complete."

"It's fine, Carl. This was a surprise trip. Do you mind excusing us?" I ask him.

He looks between the two of us and grabs his tools and walks out the front door. "Sure. I'll be back to finish tomorrow."

I nod my head at him, and then look back at Krissy.

She's looking at everything with pure awe in her face.

"How did you do this? How did you know?" she asks me. "Everything, oh my God, everything I wanted is here."

I walk slowly toward her and her eyes widen the closer I get. I use my thumbs to dry her cheeks. "Krissy, I fell in love with you in high school. But I was always the nerd with glasses and I didn't have the guts to ask you out then. I haven't been able to get you off my mind since then. So, yes, the last four years of your life, I have tried my best to help you reach your dreams. I've never gotten you anything you didn't deserve or cheated so you could get an award. I just did little things to help you."

"But how? How did you know?" she asks me, gesturing around the room.

"Your Pinterest board. You have a wish list. I got it all for you." I shrug. "I wanted you to have everything you ever wanted."

She walks away from me and looks around the room. I can tell she's deep in thought, and I try not to force myself on her. But being this close to her and not touching her is killing me.

"Well, I have almost everything I want." She walks back toward me.

"There's more in the back, but whatever you want, we'll get it," I promise her.

"What I want doesn't cost any money." She lifts her shoulder.

"Honey, I want you to have everything... whatever that is. Tell me what it is and I'll get it for you." If I'm reading her right, I can feel her softening and hope flares in my chest.

She nods her head. "Good. I want you, Jared. That's all I want. All I'll ever need. Just you."

A huge smile takes over my whole face. "You already have that. Forever."

# Epilogue

## Three Months Later

*Jared*

She's sitting in the office of her studio, stressed to the max and tears are falling down her face. She doesn't hear me come in until I'm gathering her in my arms and sitting down with her in my lap.

"What's wrong, honey?" I ask her, but I already know what it is.

"I don't know. I'm so stressed out. I'm planning this wedding and I was trying to take the pictures today of this sweet baby, and I couldn't stop crying. I'm a mess and I don't know why." She sobs into my shoulder.

"Are you happy, Krissy? Happy with me?" I ask her hesitantly.

"What? Of course I am. You make me happier than I've ever been in my life," she whispers and starts sobbing again.

I rub her back. "Can I tell you something, honey?"

She nods her head against me. "What?"

"You're pregnant, baby. You're going to be a momma!" I tell her softly.

"What?" she exclaims, looking up at me.

"Honey, you've been so busy with everything, but you've only had your period one time since we've been together. I'm pretty sure you're pregnant." I smile and kiss her lips.

"How do you even know that?"

I laugh. "I know everything when it comes to you."

And then it must hit her. "Oh my God, Jared, we're going to have a baby. I have been crying a lot, and my boobs have been sore—oh my, I am pregnant."

I soothe my hand across her swollen breasts, feeling their heaviness in my hands. I simply nod my head at her, trying to stifle the emotion I'm feeling. I can't imagine my life getting any better than it is right now.

"I love you, Krissy."

"So, uh, you're happy, I mean about the baby?" she asks me worriedly. "I know it's soon."

I run my hand across her belly and then kiss her lips softly. "I'm happy we're having a baby." I kiss her again, cupping her face in my hands and forcing her to look into my eyes. "As long as I have you by my side, I'm happy, honey."

A smile finally forms on her lips. "I love you too."

# Free Books

Want FREE BOOKS?

Go to www.authorhopeford.com/freebies

# JOIN ME!

## JOIN MY NEWSLETTER & READERS GROUP

www.AuthorHopeFord.com/Subscribe

## JOIN MY READERS GROUP ON FACEBOOK

www.FB.com/groups/hopeford

Find Hope Ford at www.authorhopeford.com

# About the Author

USA Today Bestselling Author Hope Ford writes short, steamy, sweet romances. She loves tattooed, alpha men, instant love stories, and ALWAYS happily ever afters. She has over 100 books and they are all available on Amazon.

To find me on Pinterest, Instagram, Facebook, Goodreads, and more:

www.AuthorHopeFord.com/follow-me

Printed in Great Britain
by Amazon